May's Danger

A Larry Macklin Mystery-Book 7

A. E. Howe

Books in the Larry Macklin Mystery Series:

November's Past (Book 1)

December's Secrets (Book 2)

January's Betrayal (Book 3)

February's Regrets (Book 4)

March's Luck (Book 5)

April's Desires (Book 6)

May's Danger (Book 7)

Copyright © 2017 A. E Howe

ISBN: 0-9862733-9-2
ISBN-13: 978-0-9862733-9-1

DEDICATION

With much appreciation and thanks, this one is for
Reginald D. Jordan, DVM, Ivan T. Barineau, DVM,
Larry Helm, DVM, Beth May, DVM, Nancy A. Goyert,
DVM, Dale Weeks and all the other doctors and staff who
have helped to keep our many critters healthy and happy
over the years.

CHAPTER ONE

My phone rang as I was getting out of the shower. Hearing "The Longest Time," I knew immediately that it was my girlfriend, Cara Laursen. I groaned as I hastily grabbed a towel. If she was calling me this soon after leaving for work, then it could only mean that her car had broken down, she'd forgotten her purse or something else equally inconvenient. The real reason for her call never crossed my mind.

I hurried into the bedroom, still dripping wet and almost falling as I tripped over two boxes of clothes Cara had yet to unpack. Alvin, her Pug, and my tabby cat, Ivy, watched from their perch on the bed, no doubt amused by the creative string of curse words I was uttering. I managed to grab the phone off of the nightstand just before the call went to voicemail.

"Larry, there's a dead body in the clinic."

Standing in my bedroom, mostly naked and still not fully awake, I wasn't prepared to hear those words from Cara. My mind struggled to make sense of what she was saying, but before I could ask any questions, my phone started making more noise. Holding it out, I saw that I had an incoming call from the sheriff's office. Oddly, seeing that number helped to clarify things.

"You called 911?"

"Yes," Cara said, and now I could hear the shock in her quivering voice.

"I'm getting a call from dispatch now. Are you outside? Somewhere safe?"

"I'm in my car. They wanted me to stay on the line, but I told them I was going to call you."

I was fumbling around, trying to put on my underwear while I talked with her. "I still need to get dressed. It'll be about half an hour before I can get there," I said, searching for my pants. "Look, I've got to hang up, but I'm on my way." I could hear sirens over the phone. "Can you see a patrol car?"

"Yes, they're almost here."

"I'll be there as soon as I can. Love you."

I took the call from dispatch and explained that I already knew and was on the way.

When I pulled up to the curb outside of Dr. Barnhill's veterinary clinic, I was pleased to see that the responding deputies had already cordoned off the area as a crime scene. Cara was sitting sideways in her car in the parking lot, talking with Deputy Julio Ortiz, one of the most dependable guys in the department. I went straight over to them.

"Have you been inside?" I asked Julio as I walked up.

"Definitely dead, lying in the hallway between two of the exam rooms. I took pictures as I went. Our crime scene techs and the coroner's team are on the way."

"Good job. Why don't you go direct the response?" I said.

Julio nodded and headed back to the curb to make sure that no one tried to pull into the lot or come across the lawn. You couldn't assume that, just because the area was draped with four-inch-wide, bright yellow crime scene tape, people wouldn't go over it or under it. Hell, sometimes it was our own responders who were the worst offenders.

I kneeled down beside Cara. "Did you recognize the

body?"

"No, but I couldn't see his face very well. He was lying on his stomach. It's not anyone who works here."

She was trembling a little and I put my hand on her knee to steady her nerves. "Are you all right?"

"I think so. But… it's just such a shock."

"Did you see anyone leave the building when you came up? Or loitering outside?"

"No, and I would have 'cause there's never anyone around before eight. I'm sure I'd have noticed."

"Was the alarm on when you got here?"

"Funny… Now that you mention it, I know that I went in and pushed the buttons on the alarm, but I don't think it was on. Larry, I really need to get back in there to check on all the animals and start walking the dogs," she said, referring to the clinic's regular overnight collection of boarders and animals recovering from surgeries or illness.

"I'm sorry, but they'll have to wait a little longer."

"But we've got two cats who need medicine and a Bassett that's sick…" Her voice was becoming shrill with anxiety. I took her by the shoulders and stopped her.

"Cara, look at me. It's going to be okay. I promise you, as soon as Shantel and Marcus get here, I'll go through the back with you so you can check on all the animals. Okay?"

I pulled her to me and gave her a hug. I could feel her shaking, almost hyperventilating, but as I held her she regained control. She sniffed a couple of times and then sat back up.

"I'm better. I just need to make sure they're all okay."

I saw the crime scene van roll up to the curb. "They're here. It'll be just a few more minutes. Did you notice anything else out of place? Was the door locked?"

"I don't know. I just put my key in the door like normal and turned it. I didn't try the door first. I didn't notice anything, but I went in the front door and never got past the first hallway."

"Do you always go in the front door?"

"The light switches for most of the building are in that first hallway, so it's just the most convenient way to go. And all of the notes and charts for the animals in recovery are on the door. That way I can check them and know what to expect before opening the door and getting them all excited."

"Were the lights on or off?"

"Off. I'm pretty sure about that."

Cara seemed to be focusing better. Questioning a witness can sometimes calm them down. But memory is a funny thing and you don't always get the best information from a witness right away. At first, their mind remembers events through the tunnel vision of adrenaline. But, given time, their brain will remember the experience more like it actually happened and less how their pumped-up nerves experienced events. Of course, it helps if their memory is allowed to recover organically over a couple of days without being influenced by outside information.

Leaving Cara, I went over and explained the situation to Shantel Williams and Marcus Brown, our two best crime scene techs. They made quick work of their examination of the back of the clinic, and within half an hour Cara and a kennel tech who had just shown up were taking care of the animals in the boarding area.

From all appearances, neither the victim nor the killer had entered the area where the animals were. The back door had been locked and the windows were intact and secured with iron bars on the outside. Veterinary clinics, like doctors' offices, are often targeted by addicts looking for drugs, so most of them have decent security. I had high hopes that we'd be able to use that fact to make quick work of this case. I thought it was possible that a couple of addicts had broken in and gotten into a fight, resulting in one of them lying on the floor in a pool of his own blood. It wouldn't be the first time that a falling out between crooks had resulted in a murder.

My partner, Darlene Marks, called to check in with me. I

told her to take her time getting to the scene. Everything was under control and it would be a little while before we'd have a chance to get in and look at the body. As I hung up, the van from the coroner's office drove up. I gave Dr. Darzi's assistants the same speech and we settled in to wait on Shantel and Marcus.

Thirty minutes later, having finished with their photos and video of the entire scene, they gave us the high sign. Darlene arrived just before we reached the clinic's front door.

Inside, everything looked normal, as far as I could tell. We went past reception, through a door and into the hallway where we could see a body splayed out on the floor. I moved closer, looking for anything—a footprint, a smudge on the wall, a dropped pencil. But all I saw was a white male dressed in cargo pants and a polo shirt, lying in a small puddle of blood. Had he been stabbed? Shot? Clearly the blood was coming from his front side as there were no exit wounds on his back.

I leaned down and tried to get a look at his face. Adams County was small and anyone working in law enforcement quickly learned the identities of most of our bad guys. Half the time, if you didn't know them, then you at least knew their family. But looking at the guy laid out on the floor, I got nothing. He appeared to be in his thirties and had blond hair. His face looked good—no obvious signs of drug use. Meth addicts were the worst. But this guy seemed pretty healthy. Except, of course, for the fact that he was dead.

"We know this guy?" Darlene asked, moving closer and peering at him.

"I don't think I've seen him before. I was just getting ready to look for a wallet."

I patted down his back pockets. Nothing. I could just reach his front one and managed to hit pay dirt, pulling out a nylon wallet. I found a Georgia driver's license for one John C. Rybeck. The picture on the license was a match for our corpse. I showed it to Darlene.

"Address up in Columbus. Look at the clothes. Could be military or ex-military," Darlene suggested.

Cargo pants and surplus boots weren't that unusual, but coupled with an address in a military town like Columbus, it gave us a big maybe. Fort Benning accounted for a lot of guys between twenty and forty in the Columbus area. According to the victim's license, he was thirty-two years old.

"No military ID," I said, flipping through the wallet and finding only credit cards and insurance cards. There was also about a hundred bucks in cash.

Dr. Darzi's people had been watching us patiently. "All yours," I told them as Darlene and I stepped back.

After they'd taken the body's temperature and wrapped the hands and boots in bags to preserve trace evidence, they carefully turned the body over.

"Wow!" Darlene said.

"Didn't see that coming," I said, equally surprised. The blood that had pooled around him and soaked the front of his shirt came from a blood bag crushed underneath him. Stuck in his chest was the needle of a large syringe. I called Marcus back over to take more pictures. We were worried that moving the body, no matter how carefully, would dislodge it.

"I think we should remove the needle," suggested one of Darzi's assistants. "If we put him in a body bag, we're liable to pull it out or bend it. We'd risk losing any of the liquid that's still in the body or the needle of the syringe."

"Agreed," I said. "And you'd better take the blood bag for testing too."

Both of them nodded and went about their business as professionally as a dead body would allow them. I'd seen some pretty awkward dances with corpses over the years as some resisted all efforts to be put in a body bag.

"I've got a question. Why leave the wallet?" I asked Darlene as we stood by and watched the guys work. Other than the wallet, the rest of his pockets had been empty. No keys and no phone. "I understand the killer taking the cell phone—it could have incriminating texts or messages on it. Also the keys. Maybe they came in the same car. But why leave his wallet?"

"I'll take 'Criminals Are Stupid' for 500, Alex."

"There's always that," I agreed. "We can subpoena John Rybeck's phone records and get most of the information that's on the phone."

"Unless he had a burner phone."

"That's possible. But this guy looks like he should have his own phone too."

"It's early days," Darlene said with a little smile. "You can go out and see about your girlfriend if you want. I'll finish up in here."

CHAPTER TWO

Cara was standing outside with a group that included Dr. Barnhill, several other employees of the clinic, and a few clients with appointments who'd shown up not realizing what had happened. Cara looked calm as she talked with the others. I'd told her not to discuss what she'd seen with anyone else until we'd had a chance to question them. I gave her an encouraging smile as I walked up.

"Dr. Barnhill, could I talk with you by my car?" I said to the older man. His normally smiling face was lined with concern.

"Of course," he said and followed me. "I can't believe this. Was he trying to steal drugs?"

"At this point, we don't know much," I said when we'd reached my car. "Who has keys to the clinic?"

"Several people. Myself, my wife, our office manager Sandra and whoever is going to walk and feed the animals first thing in the morning. So that would be Cara, Terry, Scott or Angie, depending on the schedule. We also have an extra set near the back door."

"So, in other words, everyone at the office has one."

"Yeah, I guess you're right."

I stifled a sigh. That meant that any of them could have

made copies. *At this point, anyone in the county could have a key*, I thought.

"These same people also have the code to the alarm?"

"Of course."

I'd taken a picture of Rybeck's driver's license with my phone. I opened the image and zoomed in so that only his photo was showing. I didn't want to give out the man's identity yet.

"Do you know this man, or have you ever seen him?" I asked.

Dr. Barnhill took out his reading glasses and peered at the image. "No, I don't think so. But I'm not very good with faces. Dogs and cats I recognize, people not so much." He gave me a sad smile.

Next I showed him a picture of the blood bag. "Is this from your clinic?"

"Possibly. We keep a couple of bags of cat and dog blood on hand for transfusions." He sounded very confused. "Why would anyone take that?"

I wondered the same thing. "Where do you keep the clinic's blood supply?"

"In the refrigerator in the drug room."

"I'm going to need for you to walk me through the drug room and tell me if anything is missing."

"We keep the narcotics in a lock box. And there's a log. I'll be able to tell you exactly what's missing from those supplies."

We went in the back door to avoid the murder scene. As we passed through the kennel, Dr. Barnhill stopped and talked to several of the animals. "How soon do you think I can get back to work?"

"We're going to need most of today to collect evidence."

"I guess I can arrange something with one of the vets in Tallahassee. Some of my patients can't wait."

"We'll do what we can to help."

"I appreciate that. I can't understand any of this."

The drug room was very neat and orderly. Dr. Barnhill

entered a digital combination which opened the large locked cabinet where they kept the controlled substances. Everything appeared to be in order. It took him the better part of half an hour to check all of the drugs and compare them to the log book.

"I don't see anything missing."

"Who has the combination to this safe?"

"Just me and my wife. I open it in the morning and it stays open all day."

"Where's the monitor for your security cameras?" *Let me have a little luck and find everything captured on video*, I prayed to Saint Columbo, the patron saint of detectives.

"Around here in my office," Dr. Barnhill said, turning down the hall before I could stop him. He put on the brakes when he saw Darzi's attendants wheeling the body bag out on a stretcher. He looked down, saw the blood and turned quickly into his office. I didn't bother to tell him that the blood probably didn't belong to the victim.

Inside his office, he pointed to a computer with a couple of monitors. "I just kind-of-sort-of understand all this. My nephew set it up for me."

"Okay, don't touch anything," I ordered as he reached out to turn the monitor on. "We'll get our IT guy to pull all the information off of it."

I didn't want him accidentally hitting a button and destroying data. And, honestly, I just knew the basics, so there was no way that I was going to touch the equipment. I put in a quick call to Lionel West, who told me that he was on his way. I was glad that we had finally hired an IT guy who had a background in forensic work.

"Where are your cameras?"

Dr. Barnhill showed me six different cameras scattered both in and outside the building. None of them were pointed at the hallway directly, but the coverage was good enough that with some luck we should have had a good picture of our suspect.

An hour later, I was standing next to Lionel and looking for the nearest wall to bang my head against.

"Someone turned the system off around two in the morning," Lionel said. "Here's the logout time." He pointed to the second-to-last entry on the screen.

"Of course it was turned off. What fun would it be if we could just show everyone a picture of the killer?" Darlene asked. Sarcasm was a specialty of hers.

"That's not all the bad news," Lionel continued. "Looks like some footage has been erased. There's nothing here after six last night."

I turned to Dr. Barnhill. "Who could have turned off the security cameras?"

"You mean, who had the knowledge?"

"Yes. We'll worry about who was here at two in the morning later."

"I would guess that just about anyone could have figured it out. It's not that hard. My nephew showed me, my wife and Sandra how to turn it on and off, and how to review the footage. But we've had problems with it a few times and then just about everyone has tried to help me with it. You know how that is. None of us really knows what's wrong or how it works, but everyone wants to try to help. Usually we end up calling Howie. That's my nephew." He gave me Howie's contact information.

Darlene and I did quick, perfunctory interviews with the rest of the staff on hand. When did you leave the office? When did you come in? Do you know the victim? Can you imagine any reason why someone would have removed a unit of blood? All of the answers were in the negative. Once we had some idea of why John Rybeck was in the clinic, then we'd have to bring everyone back for more detailed questioning.

At midday, Dr. Barnhill and the other techs transported all the animals that couldn't go home over to a clinic in Tallahassee. Cara stayed behind to help the clients that showed up when no one could reach them by phone, or the ones that had a hard time getting to Tallahassee. Being a rural county, our population tended to skew older. A number of Dr. Barnhill's clients were over seventy. Cara was doing triage and making sure that the ones whose pets needed to see a doctor immediately were able to drive to Tallahassee or could get a ride.

"How are you holding up?" I asked her when she finally got a break. She was leaning against her car, holding her cell phone. All of the clinic's numbers had been forwarded to hers.

"I'm okay. I think I've finally talked with all of the appointments we had on the books for the next two days."

"Why isn't Gayle handling the calls?" I asked. Gayle was the receptionist.

"She took a couple days off to go to Atlanta with her boyfriend. Lucky her."

I made a note to check up on Gayle's alibi. Cara leaned in for a quick kiss, then told me that she was heading to Tallahassee to help out at the other clinic.

I checked with the Georgia DMV and learned that John drove a ten-year-old silver Nissan Sentra with Georgia plates. I put out a BOLO on it after Darlene and I scoured the area around the clinic without success. Whoever killed him had most likely moved the car.

Next we did quick interviews with the businesses on either side of Dr. Barnhill's office—a chiropractor and a beauty salon. No one had come in early today or been around late yesterday at either business, and no one could report seeing or hearing anything odd. The chiropractor did have a security camera that caught a corner of the street and he gave me a copy of the last twenty-four hours of footage on a thumb drive to take back to Lionel.

It was almost four when Shantel and Marcus finally packed up their van and Darlene followed them back to the office. Before I could join them, dispatch contacted me with a phone number for John Rybeck's parents. They lived in

Tennessee.

"Mr. Rybeck?" I asked the man who answered the phone.

"It is. Can I help you?" The voice had a distinct mountain twang.

"This is Deputy Larry Macklin with the Adams County Sheriff's Office in Florida. I'm afraid that I have some very bad news."

"Oh, God!" It wasn't simply an exclamation, but obviously a request to God that this call not be what he feared.

"Is John Rybeck your son? Living in Columbus, Georgia?" I wasn't intentionally torturing the man by dragging out my questions, but a death notification is not something you want to deliver by mistake.

"Yes, he is, and he does, yes." All of the strength had gone out of his voice.

"I'm sorry to inform you that your son was found dead this morning in a veterinary clinic in the city of Calhoun, Florida."

"A... a veterinary clinic?" I could hear a bit of hope coming back into the man's tone. "John doesn't have any pets."

"I don't think he was there to get treatment for an animal. He was in the building after hours."

"I see," he said. *What does he see?* I wondered.

"Do you have any idea why he might have been in the clinic?"

There was a heavy sigh on the other end of the line. "No, I don't, but I'm sure that you'll run his name through your computer and find out that he's been in trouble with the law in the past. He hung around the wrong people when he was younger. Liked to be the hero. One time he got into a fight with some gal's boyfriend because the boyfriend was pushing her around. Turned out, she didn't appreciate John's help." He paused, the memories of his son overwhelming him for a moment. Finally he continued, "What... How did he die?"

"I honestly can't say at this time. We'll be performing an

autopsy and that should give us a few more answers."

"I can't quite take this all in. I guess I need to know when we can get the body for burial. I'll have to talk to Raymond at the funeral home. My wife… She's not here right now… I can't imagine how I'm going to tell her. We have two daughters, but she's always doted on that boy. She'll want to come down there. Can I call you back when I know what we're doing?" he asked, sounding unsure.

"Of course, Mr. Rybeck. It would be a big help if you could give us some detailed information on your son."

"We'll probably be down there tomorrow, or the next day at the latest."

"You can just call me when you have a better idea," I said and made sure that he had my name and number.

He was right about his son's record. I'd pulled it up on my laptop and saw a number of interactions with law enforcement and a few arrests. The arrests were in several different towns in Georgia and Alabama. Once I read the reports, I knew it should cast more light on who John Rybeck was and how his life had ended in a veterinary clinic in north Florida.

CHAPTER THREE

I finally got to the office a little after five, in time to see my old partner, Pete Henley, heading across the parking lot. The big guy smiled and waved.

"Heard you grabbed an interesting one," he said and then added with concern, "Is Cara all right?"

"It definitely shook her up a bit."

"Finding a dead body will do that," he said sympathetically. "How's your side?"

"It only hurts when someone mentions it," I told him with a smile, though that wasn't entirely true. I'd been stabbed barely two weeks before while helping Pete catch a serial killer who had kidnapped his daughter. The scar was still tender, but the last thing in world I wanted to do was to let Pete think that it bothered me. He'd felt guilty enough as it was.

He held up both hands. "I know I owe you one," he said, then sighed. "I could really use you back as a partner. I caught a drug deal gone bad on the south side, with both of the combatants sent to the hospital. We had to move one of them to a different hospital because he kept trying to sneak out of his room to try and kill the other one."

"Actually, something that straightforward sounds kinda

nice."

"The grass is always greener." Pete grinned and waved as he headed to his car.

I went to the evidence room to see if Shantel and Marcus had collected anything promising. They'd taken a lot of samples, but most of what they had wouldn't help us until we found a suspect. When I entered the room, they were only about half done with logging in the bags and samples.

"It wasn't like I could pick up all the hairs in that place," Shantel said in exasperation. "It would take a year just to separate out which went with what type of animal."

"Nothing jumped out at you?"

"We collected a lot of junk. Give me a suspect and maybe I'll be able to tell you whether he or she was there. Short of that, it'd just be a waste of time."

"Maybe Darzi's folks will get something from the syringe."

"First time I've seen a body with a syringe in it that wasn't an accidental overdose. Does make me wonder what was in that thing," Marcus said, then shuddered. "I hate needles."

"Hopefully Darzi will be able to tell us shortly. Ya'll want me to help?" I offered, knowing the response I'd get.

"Get out of here. That's all I'd need is for one of you oafs to start entering your half-ass labels and nonsense into my evidence logs. We'd never find anything. Go on, git!" Shantel shooed me out of the room.

It was just getting dark as I opened my gate and drove up to the house. I'd bought twenty acres with an old doublewide on it shortly after I'd started working as a deputy. Now, for the first time, I was sharing my home under the live oaks with someone else. It felt strange, but also oddly comforting, to know that this was Cara's home too. Her car was already there and the lights were on in the house.

I was greeted at the door by Alvin, who always seemed glad to see me. Ivy, who I'd rescued from the parking lot of the sheriff's office more than a year ago, was still coming to terms with the new living arrangements. She stared at me from the back of the couch, her eyes mere slits as Alvin let out a couple of little woofs to announce his pleasure that everyone was finally home.

Cara came out of the bedroom and headed straight to me, giving me a long hug. I squeezed her tight.

"How are you?"

"It was a long day, even more so trying to work in someone else's clinic, but we got everyone taken care of."

"Have you had dinner?"

"Doc bought pizza for everyone at the clinic. A little thank you for both staffs. How 'bout you?"

"I'll just fix a sandwich." I went into the kitchen and Cara followed me. As I assembled my dinner, I said, "I want to do one more walk-through of the building before you all move back in. I called Dr. Barnhill and told him to give us until noon."

"I just don't understand what someone was doing in the clinic at night. Let alone how they got themselves murdered."

I sat down at the table. "Hopefully we'll get some answers when we take a deeper look into the victim's past and the lives of his associates. The guy has a record. I don't think he was in there for no reason. Our best chance to figure it out is in his past."

"You think he was there for drugs?"

"Possibly. Maybe he thought there'd be something to steal." Even as I said it, I didn't believe it was plausible. Who would think that there'd be valuables in a veterinary clinic? Drugs, maybe. But it didn't look like there'd been any attempt to steal the drugs. There was just that weird detail of the blood bag found under the body. Of course, it's often the strange details that can help solve a case.

"I can't imagine that anyone at the clinic had anything to do with it."

"Look, I don't want to turn this into an interview, but…

21

can you think of anything odd that's happened over the last couple of weeks?"

"I can't think of anything," Cara said, her brow furrowed.

"Anybody change their routine?"

"I guess you could say that Gayle has. I mean, she's got her new boyfriend, Wayne."

"That's the idea. Tell me about the boyfriend," I encouraged her, taking a bite of my ham sandwich.

"I don't know much. He's been coming to the clinic for over a year. He's got an adorable English Bulldog named Caesar. The guy is pretty cute too," she admitted, seeming more relaxed than I'd seen her all day.

"Do tell."

"He's rugged. Kind of got a young Brad Pitt thing going on. Piercing eyes. Sloppy, but adorable hair. Looks like he works out. Always wearing clothes that are manly and almost, but not quite, too fashionable."

"Wow, so he's a lot like me."

"Exact opposite!" she said with a grin and I tossed a napkin at her. Cara laughed and held up her hands in surrender. After the day she'd had, it was good to hear her laugh.

"What about his temperament?"

The question sobered Cara up. I hadn't meant to pursue it, but something about the guy intrigued me.

"He seems nice," she said, slightly hesitant.

"But...? What's wrong with him?"

"Nothing really. Maybe... and this sounds stupid... he seems too nice. Too flirty, maybe."

"Has he always, or just recently?"

"That's a good question. You know, he's been coming in pretty regularly. Most folks, if they have a cat or a dog that's in those great years between two and ten, only come in once a year unless something pretty serious happens. But this guy, he's brought Caesar in maybe five or six times in the last year. I'd have to check his records for the exact number."

"Is Caesar sick?"

"No. I mean, Wayne brings Caesar in when he thinks something is wrong, but mostly it's just the normal ups and downs of a young dog. You know, he ate something that didn't agree with him and barfed it up. That sort of thing. So Wayne brings him in to be checked out. Which is fine, it's just a little unusual."

"You think he's coming in for another reason? Maybe he had a thing for Gayle from the beginning. He wouldn't be the first guy to come up with excuses to see a woman."

"I thought about that. Maybe…"

"What's wrong with that idea?"

"You've seen Gayle."

"Yeah. She seems nice."

"She's nice, sure, but not the kind of woman that men fall all over themselves to date." She paused and looked frustrated. "Listen to me. I know all guys aren't shallow, but…"

"But what?"

"You haven't seen Wayne. He's a good looking guy, and he's almost ten years younger than Gayle."

"Some guys go for cougars."

"Could be," Cara said, not sounding satisfied with the explanation.

I finished my sandwich and took my plate to the sink while Cara watched Alvin as he snored away after his dinner. He was lying in a bed that I'd bought for Ivy and was completely oblivious to the fact that the cat was sitting beside him, hovering like a vulture. She'd never shown an interest in the bed until Alvin had decided that he liked to snooze in it.

I came back over and put my hand on Cara's shoulder and she reached up, taking it in hers. "Someone at the clinic must have let him in," she said quietly.

I'd hadn't wanted to make a point of that, but obviously she'd figured out that the possibility of a mole inside the clinic was real.

"That's likely. Not a hundred percent, but it's probably

about ninety-five percent probable that he was aided by someone connected with the clinic. But with the way the keys are handled, it could even be a friend or relative of someone who works there."

"I'd never even thought about the clinic's security."

I guided her over to the couch. "People don't until there's a problem. I should have said something. The department will do security assessments for businesses any time they want. You'd be surprised how sloppy some of them are. For instance, the hardware store wasn't making deposits every night. They'd wait all week, keep the money in their safe, and then do one big deposit on Saturday. And when they did make the deposit, they were letting one guy carry, like, ten thousand dollars in cash, plus checks, to the bank by himself at eight or nine at night. He had to put it in a couple of envelopes just to get it through the slot of the night deposit box. Crazy. They were lucky that no one ever robbed the guy. Or that the guy making the deposit didn't get greedy."

"I just hate to think that someone I know might have been involved in this guy's murder."

"There are plenty of bad people in the world and maybe this is just someone who got caught up in trouble that got out of control. I see it every day. Good people who slide into trouble. Only a very small percentage of people are true desperados seeking to do evil."

She leaned into me for a moment, then pushed away. "I'd better get to bed. It's going to be a long day tomorrow."

"I'm glad you moved in," I said. She leaned over and we shared a long kiss. "And not just for all those benefits." I winked at her as she walked away, smiling.

CHAPTER FOUR

On Thursday, Cara and I got up before the sun. I wanted to get an early start on compiling all of the information we had on John Rybeck, hoping that it would provide me with a plan of attack for the rest of the day. As for Cara, her normally quick commute would be stretched to almost forty-five minutes as she headed for the clinic in Tallahassee.

When I walked into the office, I saw my dad standing in the hallway. Sheriff Ted Macklin was wearing a very puzzled look on his face.

"Lose something?" I asked, bemused.

"Did you see Mauser?"

Mauser was his horse-sized, two-and-a-half year-old, black-and-white Great Dane. More often than not, Dad brought the spoiled monster into the office. I think he just liked to watch people's reactions to the big baby. Or maybe it really was lonely at the top and Dad appreciated having someone that he could confide in who would never tell tales.

"What are you doing letting him run loose in the office?" I asked, not really having the time to help with a pony round-up.

"I was carrying a box of papers and I couldn't hold the door, the box and his leash all at the same time. I figured he'd be fine outside my office for ten seconds."

I was barely able to keep myself from commenting that he'd obviously been wrong, but Dad would tolerate only so much insolence. "He's got to be around here somewhere," I said instead, just as I heard hoof beats pounding down the hall.

I turned and saw Mauser loping toward us, his leash dangling between his legs and something large and black swinging from his mouth. It was one of the SWAT team's body armor vests with a fifteen-pound steel plate half hanging out of it. The dog put on a final burst of speed and came up beside me, swinging his head as though he wanted to play a game of keep-away with me. The steel plate went left and then, before I realized what was happening, swung back and slammed into my thigh hard enough to send me to the ground. I just managed to duck when it swung back for a second pass.

"Look out!" I yelled to Dad as Mauser wheeled around and trotted toward him.

I struggled to my feet, attracting Mauser's attention again. He came charging back at me, swinging his trophy and putting several sizable holes in the drywall. Not thinking very clearly, I headed toward the glass door that opened onto the office lobby, but a vision of shattered glass helped me realize my mistake just in time. I stopped and turned to face the brute, bracing for the pain of impact as he came at me, joyously swinging the weighted vest.

But nothing happened. Mauser stopped a foot in front of me, gave me an innocent look and dropped the vest, which hit the floor with a solid thud. Done wrecking havoc, the Dane eased himself to the floor, panting. His eyes were glowing with pride.

"You undisciplined monster," I told him, rubbing my thigh.

I looked over at Dad, who was trying to decide if the incident was funny or embarrassing. He settled on funny, chuckling as he came over and grabbed Mauser's leash, tugging the beast to his feet.

"Thanks a lot," I said, reaching down to pick up the vest. "You're lucky we're brothers," I told Mauser, thinking, *Unfortunately, he's the favored son.*

Dad hauled Mauser to his office while I limped a little on the way to my desk. But I'd barely started work on assembling a contact list for Rybeck when I felt someone standing behind me. I looked up to see Dad, an odd expression on his face.

"Look, Larry. You've only recently come off of light duty. Are you sure you're ready to pick up another murder investigation? I can still assign Darlene as the lead on this one if you want."

"Are you kidding?" I asked, thoroughly uncomfortable with Dad showing any amount of concern about me. "I was bored stiff doing desk work. And with this case touching so close to Cara, there's no way I'm not working on it."

Dad nodded. "Good. Wanted to make sure since you just let yourself get beat up by a puppy."

"Ha! That wasn't a puppy, it was your one-hundred-and-ninety-pound domesticated rhino. Not the same thing at all. I'm fine. Don't worry about me."

"Who said I was worried about you? I just don't want anything screwing up the investigation."

With the usual tenor of our relationship restored, Dad returned to his office. Darlene walked up a few minutes later, a list of Dr. Barnhill's employees in her hand.

"Gayle is supposed to be back in town this afternoon. We should be able to interview all of his staff by tomorrow," she said.

"I'm interested in her boyfriend. Cara made their relationship sound pretty hinky."

"His full name is Wayne Dawson. Lives on a small farm about ten miles from town. I ran him and he's clean."

I told Darlene what Cara had said about his behavior.

"Love is a many splendored thing. And dating below yourself is not unheard of. Look at Cara," she said with a grin.

"I do acknowledge that Cara is dating below her class in looks. But what I lack in looks, I make up for in charm."

"If you say so. Maybe Gayle is good at other things," Darlene said suggestively.

"I'll be sure to question Wayne about all aspects of their relationship."

We started making phone calls. I contacted all of the law enforcement agencies that had arrested John Rybeck over the years and requested that they send me copies of their reports. Then I tried calling numbers that I'd found in a random assortment of Internet searches, hoping to find someone that would admit to knowing him. After a couple of misses, I finally got ahold of a neighbor, Duke Waters.

"Yeah, I live next door. Where'd you say you were again?"

I explained again where and who I was.

"And you want to know about John?" The guy sounded like a senior citizen. "Why?"

"We're just conducting a standard background check." I didn't want to tell him that Rybeck was dead. People can get funny when they know that someone has died, and even more so if the person was killed. They either don't want to sound like they had a reason to want the person dead, or they just don't want to speak ill of the dead. Either way, I wanted to find out what people thought of John Rybeck when he was alive.

"He's a real nice guy. I hope he isn't in any trouble."

"We don't know yet exactly how he's involved." Which was the truth.

"I'm a Vietnam veteran and I'll tell you that John is always very respectful and helps me when he can. I got some problems with my legs and a couple of times he's taken me to the hospital. Damn government doesn't do shit for me. You tell him that if there's anything I can do for him, he should just call."

"Do you know where he worked?"

"Can't you ask him?" the old man said and I began to feel bad about putting on a charade.

"We're just verifying his employment," I said evasively.

"Odd jobs, mostly. He did work for a couple of guys. I seen 'em around. Not very nice or polite."

"Do you know their names?"

"I don't know… maybe Martin? Mario? Some damn name like that. Ask John."

"Do you know of any other people that I could talk to about him? A girlfriend or roommate?"

He chuckled. "He had a bunch of girls at different times. Nice tits and ass, all of them. Best part of having John as a neighbor was the women who hung around," he said gleefully, sounding like the classic dirty old man.

"Do you have any of their names or phone numbers?"

"Hell, I wish I did." More laughter. "Wait. Damn it, I do have a number for one of them." I could hear the man shuffling through some papers. "John gave me a name and number when he dropped me off at the doctor's one time. I called it when I got done. Her name's Cherry." He gave me the number.

"Why'd he give you her number and not his?"

"I think he said his phone wasn't working, or he'd lost it. I forget. My blood sugar was in the gutter. Makes me kinda wacky. That's why I had to go to the doctor."

"When was the last time you saw John?"

"Guess it's been about a week."

"Is that normal?"

"Hell, yeah. He comes and goes. Like I said, he grabs work where he can."

I thanked him for his service and was ready to hang up when he said, "Tell John I hope everything's okay." He paused for a second and then added, "I miss seeing him."

I couldn't keep the truth from the old guy any longer. I explained the situation, but asked him not to spread the word just yet and apologized for not telling him the truth right away.

"I understand. I hope you get the bastard that did this. John may have had problems, but I could tell he was a good guy. You get where you can tell. There are people walking around acting like butter wouldn't melt in their mouths, but they're really nasty as a pit viper. And then there are guys like John—a little rough around the edges, but they got a good heart. May he rest in peace."

I hung up the phone feeling a bit more sympathetic toward John Rybeck.

I called Cherry next, not really expecting to get an answer. I figured, from the name she was using and the company she was keeping, that the number probably went to a pay-as-you-go phone. But, to my surprise, a peppy voice answered on the second ring.

"Cherry here. Hope you have money," she said, not changing my mental image of her at all.

"I have a little," I answered, thinking that playing along for a minute might answer a question or two.

"Oh, honey, I'll make you wish you had more. Now what can I do for you?"

"What can you do for me?" I threw the ball back in her court.

"You're a playa, I can tell. First, why don't you tell me where you got my number."

"I got it from John Rybeck."

"How is John?"

I thought of a number of snappy answers. Finally, I settled on, "He's doing as well as can be expected."

"Yeah, hard-up John. What's your name?"

"Larry."

"Well, Larry, I don't like to do a lot of talking. I'm more into action. And if you have the cash, we should get down to business."

I'd started down this road, but now I wasn't sure where to find the exit ramp. "Tell me where to meet you."

She gave me an address in Phenix City, Alabama, which was just across the river from Columbus.

"Will you wait for me?" I asked, trying to sound lascivious. She assured me that she would and I told her to give me half an hour. I figured that was the most I could string her along.

I hung up with Cherry and got on the phone with the Phenix City police. I was wishing that I'd set something up ahead of time, but how could I have known which jurisdiction she was in? However, after only ten minutes, I had a Phenix City investigator who was willing to help a brother out.

Forty-five minutes later, I was getting some FaceTime with Cherry. She was sitting in the backseat of a police car, and was either over-dressed or under-dressed, depending on your point of view. She looked a bit more like a college girl trying to pay her rent than a crack whore, but it was hard to tell through the phone.

"Thanks a lot," she said sarcastically.

"I'm sorry, but I thought you might not talk to me if you knew I was an investigator."

"Damn right! Isn't there a law against cops lying?"

"No. No, there really isn't," I told her. "Which, in your current line of work, might be information you can use."

It was obvious that she wanted to tell me to go hang myself, but she looked around and apparently decided that it was better to hear me out.

"So what was so important?" she asked, pouting.

"First things first. Your real name is Caroline Doyle, right?" The Phenix City investigator had given me her stats before he'd turned the phone over to her.

"Forget it. Call me Cherry."

I confirmed her current address, then asked, "How well do you know John Rybeck?"

From her expression, I could tell that she was more interested now. "We've partied together a few times," she said, then added, "He's nicer than most of the Army jerks."

"But he's not in the Army. Does he hang around with guys who are in the Army?"

"Bunch of the party guys around here are from Fort Benning. So, yeah, he hangs with the party crowd."

"In Phenix City?"

"Yeah, sometimes."

"And you helped his neighbor out one time?"

"What? Oh, the old guy. Yeah, sure. Like I said, John's different. He, like, noticed the old guy and wanted to help him. John said the dude had been in some war or something. John was really impressed by him. He talked me into picking him up at the hospital once. It was okay. I didn't like having the guy in my car 'cause he smelled a little bad, but John said he needed help."

"What does John do for a living?" I was still using the present tense, figuring that she already thought I was a liar.

"This and that."

"I need more of an answer than that."

"I'm not getting John in trouble. I told you, he's okay." From her expression it was obvious that she meant it. Being in a cop car had intimidated her for a moment, but from the clam routine I was guessing that she had dealt with the law often enough not to be too bothered by it.

"I've got some bad news about John," I said, deciding that I needed to level with her if I wanted to get any more information out of her. Since she had liked John, maybe she'd want to help find his murderer. "He was killed here in Adams County."

Her mouth fell open and stuck that way for a moment. Just when I thought I was going to have to prompt her, she spoke. "You're a liar. I don't believe it."

"I'm being straight with you now. I want to find the person who did this. If you were his friend then you should want to help too."

Cherry looked down, obviously more upset than she wanted to admit. I gave her a minute to recover.

"He was the nicest guy I've met here," she finally said in small voice. "I don't want him to be dead." It sounded like the heartfelt wish of a child, a lost girl under all the makeup.

32

My respect for the dead man was growing. He'd obviously been a good enough person to touch this woman's heart.

"I'm sorry your friend is gone," I told her. "If I'm going to find his murderer, I need information. Will you help me?"

"I don't know much," she said, wiping at her eyes.

"That puts you ahead of me. Right now I don't know *anything* about John. Whatever you can tell me will help. First, how did he make money?"

I saw her bite her lower lip. "Look, some of the guys he worked for... I can't get myself in trouble. I can't afford to go into hiding or anything." I could hear real fear in her voice and see it in her eyes.

"Okay, for right now, all I'm asking is what he did. Not who he did it for. When we get done talking, I want you to give the investigator that picked you up the names of the people John worked for. Not what he did, specifically, just their names. If later it looks like this is an avenue that we have to go down, I'll get with you and we'll figure out how to protect you. But, for right now, we won't put the names and the work together. How does that sound?"

I could tell that she still wasn't sure, but gradually she started to look more angry than frightened. "I don't know any of the details. But him, and some of the other guys he hung out with, did some security stuff for guys who were... you know... buying and selling... stuff." She was trying every way she could not to say the word "drugs." If it made her more willing to talk, then I was fine with her euphemisms.

"What are we talking about? Street stuff or something bigger?"

"Really, I don't know a lot. He'd go away for a couple of days and come back with money."

"So it wasn't local?"

"I don't think so. I wouldn't see any of them for a few days and then, when they'd show up, it was party time."

"Have you seen any of these guys in the last few days?"

"Yeah, now that you say it. I didn't think about it when

John didn't call. I figured he'd gone off with them, but yesterday I saw Dou... one of them."

"Did you speak to him?"

"No, we were at a bar. I had someone with me who was paying. We made eye contact, and he raised his glass to say hi."

"Did he seem like he was acting weird or odd?"

"No. He was drinking with some other people. Hard to say if he was with them or if they just met at the bar."

"But it was just the one guy. You didn't see any of the others?"

"No, but that's not too strange. They didn't always hang out together."

"Did you ever hear John say anything about Calhoun, Florida?"

"No. He talked a lot, but I don't remember him ever mentioning Calhoun. He talked about going down to Panama City. I think he went down there to party some. But he never invited me." There was some regret in her voice.

"Did the other guys go down to Panama City with him?"

"I don't know."

"Do you think they ever came down to Florida to do their security work?"

"Honestly, I kind of thought they might have been going down to the coast somewhere. Maybe New Orleans, Mobile. Maybe Texas. But I just thought that because that's where you think of dr... stuff coming from."

"They never talked about their security work?"

"No. Even when they were drunk, they never said where all the money came from. I remember another girl asking about it too. One of the guys got real nasty with her after that. I kinda took that as a clue not to ask nothin'."

"Where did John live?"

"I don't know the address, but it's on—"

"I don't care about the address. I mean, what type of place did he live in?" I'd already contacted the Columbus Police Department and asked them to send someone to

Rybeck's apartment to secure it. Also, I'd done ye ole Google Maps drive-by. I was thinking that a trip up there to check it out might be in order, depending on the autopsy report.

"It's an apartment. Not too good of a neighborhood, but not bad. A lot of Army guys stay there. Some wives and stuff. Ones that don't or can't live on the base."

I got the names and contact information of a few people that she was comfortable mentioning, then she put the investigator on the phone. I thanked him and made sure that he wouldn't give Cherry a hard time.

CHAPTER FIVE

I had a voicemail from Rybeck's parents. They would be in town tomorrow. I wondered how much they had known about their son's recent lifestyle. I was betting not much.

Several of John's arrest reports had arrived in my email. It was all pretty basic stuff. He had never resisted arrest, getting into trouble mainly because he was careless and/or dumb. All of which indicated to me that he wasn't the brains behind the break-in at Dr. Barnhill's. There were half a dozen possible contacts in the arrest reports, but I'd have to wait to follow-up on them. Darlene was looking at her watch and pointing in the general direction of the clinic.

We got there about ten-thirty. "I wish I'd come over last night," Darlene said. "To have seen it the way our victim and his killer did."

She had a good point. The look and feel of a place can vary, depending on the time of day. Different people, different sounds. You might notice something at night that you didn't see during the day, or vice versa.

We went in through the front door. I was almost one hundred percent sure they'd come in that way. It was less likely to get the dogs all stirred up, and since they'd probably had help from the inside, then why not come in the front door?

We looked at all the windows, none of which looked like they'd been opened in years. Nothing appeared disturbed near the reception area. There hadn't been any shoeprints on the tile floor and Marcus had thoroughly dusted all the surfaces. He'd picked up dozens of prints, but they'd have to wait until we had a suspect to match them to.

"No gloves," I said, thinking about how John supposedly broke into the clinic, but that he hadn't been wearing any gloves when we'd found him.

"You're right." Darlene nodded. "Did John just not bother or, more oddly, did the killer remove them?"

"I'm beginning to think that John, and maybe the killer, never planned on taking anything. They didn't break in and weren't planning on stealing anything, so why wear gloves?"

"Then why was John here?"

"To meet someone?"

"Or to leave something."

"Or to take something that wouldn't be missed, like data," I suggested.

Darlene shrugged. "Maybe Rybeck was planning to visit the clinic during business hours, so he wasn't worried about not having an excuse for leaving trace evidence."

"Possibly…"

"It seems pretty certain that there *was* an inside person."

"Looks like there had to be. The question is, are the murderer and the insider one and the same person?"

"Fair enough. I think we should look for a connection between Rybeck and our inside man or woman."

"We can start by cross-referencing his background with those of all the people who have access to the clinic."

"Do you think Cara can withstand the scrutiny?" Darlene joked.

"I'm not too worried about her. But I'll let you check out her parents," I said with a laugh. Cara's parents were a bit unusual—hippies at heart, but her father had a healthy dose of Viking warrior thrown in for good measure.

A. E. HOWE

We finished up at the clinic and I called Dr. Barnhill to let him know that they could move back in. As we were walking out, I said, "You know, if the murderer and the fifth columnist are the same person, then we're wasting our time even worrying about fingerprints and trace evidence."

"But we *don't* know," Darlene said, stating the apparent motto of this investigation.

Dr. Darzi had scheduled Rybeck's autopsy for one o'clock. As Adams County was too small to have its own hospital, our coroner worked out of one in Tallahassee. When we got to the morgue, I found a piece of cardboard with my name on it where some wit had taped it to the door.

"You are here almost as much as I am," Dr. Darzi said, his light Indian accent laced with humor.

"You guys are a riot around here," I told him.

We had to wait almost half an hour while they finished up with a grossly obese man who had died of a heart attack. But since he'd been behind the wheel of his car when it had happened, an autopsy was required. As his assistants wheeled the large man out, Dr. Darzi moved to the table where John Rybeck was laid out and waved me over.

"Thankfully for you, I'm not an idiot. We've already tested the remains in the syringe for the most common drugs used in veterinary medicine. It was acepromazine, a sedative used on dogs. I wouldn't be surprised if we find out that's what killed our victim."

"How quickly would that have killed him?"

"Looking at where the puncture wound is, I'd guess that it went directly into his heart. He would have died almost instantly."

"Wouldn't anything injected into his heart have killed him?" Darlene asked.

"Yes. I imagine the sedative was insurance in case they missed the heart."

Darzi begin a meticulous inspection of the body. When he got to Rybeck's face, he stopped and looked at it from several different angles.

"What do you see?" I asked.

"Nothing. That's what's odd. There are no signs of trauma. Not to his face or on his arms," he said, lifting and turning each arm.

"So no defensive wounds."

"Meaning he was taken by surprise," Darlene said.

Darzi was able to establish that the syringe had injected the sedative directly into the heart.

"So the killer probably had specialized knowledge or special skill?"

Darzi looked thoughtful. "Most people know roughly where the heart is, but they either had skill or luck to miss all the ribs and the breastbone. While I don't think you can say for sure that this was someone with medical training, it *was* someone who was confident in what they were doing. I don't see any signs that they hesitated."

"That's a mighty large needle," I said with a grimace. The syringe was sitting on a metal tray close to the examination table. Darzi had used it to compare with the hole in Rybeck's chest. We had found the packaging that the syringe came in on the floor at the clinic. I assumed that it was from their inventory, but I hadn't asked Dr. Barnhill about it yet. I made a note to do that when we interviewed him and used my phone to take a close-up of the syringe.

"Can you tell anything from the angle that the needle entered his chest?" Darlene asked.

"The victim is not tall. And there is a slight downward angle to the channel created by the needle. Overhand would have been the best way to plunge the needle into the chest." He paused for a moment. "Any average-sized person would be able to inflict the wound as it is presented in the corpse. But you can probably eliminate persons over seven feet tall and under four and a half," he said with a smile.

"So Ringling Brothers is in the clear," I said. "Can you tell us anything about the victim?"

"He seems to have been in good to very good health.

There is no physical evidence that he abused drugs. Of course, we'll have to wait for the toxicology report to come back before we'll know if he had anything in his system at the time of death. He looks like an average American corpse. Actually, he's in better shape than what I normally see come through the door."

We left him to finish taking all of the samples they'd need for the lab work. During the ride back to Calhoun, we discussed strategies.

"I'd like to know more about Rybeck before we tackle Barnhill's people," I said.

"It would be nice to have a good set of questions to ask them."

"We need to ask about the needle and the security system," I said.

"And have any of them ever been to Columbus, Fort Benning or Phenix City?"

We brainstormed a few more questions, but agreed that we'd wait until tomorrow afternoon to do the interviews. That would give us the rest of the day to dig deeper into Rybeck's past and the next morning to talk with his parents.

"I think we should have pictures of everyone who works at the clinic to show to his parents. Maybe this goes back a ways. They might recognize someone," Darlene suggested.

"Good idea. Though I think the questionable work that Rybeck was doing is a more likely source for our murderer. But I'll run by the clinic later today and take everyone's picture. If I wind up having to go up to Columbus, being able to show the pictures around could come in handy." *Going by the clinic will give me a chance to check in with Cara too*, I thought.

When we got back to the office, I started calling the various departments that had sent arrest reports for Rybeck, hoping to track down some of the arresting officers to speak with them. I had to leave messages for most of them, but I did manage to get in touch with Sergeant Clayton of the

Columbus Police Department. I had to read the arrest report to him to jog his memory.

"I got it now. That fella was all right. He'd gotten into a fight with some guy that had fifty pounds on him. Seemed the guy was hitting on some woman who was tired of it, and Rybeck stepped in, but got more than he'd bargained for. The woman confirmed everything, but said Rybeck overreacted. The other guy was pretty obnoxious. I would have let Rybeck go, but he really did stir it up. The bar's owner was pissed, so I had to arrest him."

"What else do you remember about him?"

"Chatty guy. You know how it is. Some of them you can't get to talk and others you can't get to shut up. Rybeck fell into the second category. He asked me if I had been in the Army. When I told him that I was, he was real interested. I remember he told me that he'd tried to join up."

"You remember him pretty well."

"I liked the guy. Hell, he was the first collar who ever thanked me for defending the country. He seemed like a nice guy. Don't get me wrong. I'm streetwise enough to know that the nice ones can be the most dangerous, but I don't think he was like that. I asked him what he thought he was doing getting into a bar fight."

"What'd he say?"

"Said he didn't like to see guys picking on ladies. He had a knight-in-shining-armor complex bad. Also, he said he'd already screwed up his record. Apparently he got in trouble out of high school and that's why he couldn't join the Army."

"What's the bottom line on him?" I asked.

"Honestly, I've seen it before. He had a warped view of reality. Saw himself as the hero. Sooner or later, that stuff gets you into trouble if you don't have a realistic outlet for it. Get the right job and learn that those golden moments when you get to save the damsel are rare as hen's teeth and the rest of the job is boredom mixed with hard work, and you're good."

"That describes a lot of cops and firemen."

"And the military. But if you have a hero complex and don't, or can't, have the right job, you can get yourself into real trouble. That's where Rybeck was headed. Sorry to hear he got killed."

We talked for a couple more minutes and I was getting ready to hang up when he suggested that I talk to John's probation officer. I got him on the first try.

"Why are you interested in John Rybeck?" Charles Foster asked me.

"You were his probation officer?"

"Still am. He has almost six months left," Foster said.

No, he doesn't, I thought and I gave him what details I could on John's death.

"That's a shame. I had some hope for him."

"I've talked to a few people already. They all seem to agree that he was a nice guy."

"He was. John's problem was that he couldn't get into the Army. He really thought that he was meant to be a soldier. Unfortunately, he'd screwed up and gotten arrested right after high school. Since he'd turned eighteen, the prosecutor wasn't going to give him a break."

"What happened?"

"I don't know all the details. That was before I was involved with John. He's been in a little bit of trouble off and on ever since. The last time was for drunk and disorderly. When they frisked him down, he had a knife on him so he got six months for it. That's what he was serving probation for now. He got out last October."

"Did he have a job?"

"Several, but he hadn't been able to hold one down for longer than a month. He just wasn't motivated. Sad, because I think he would have made a great soldier. Of course, I don't know that. John might have gotten in and had the same problems he was having on the outside. At least he would have known. The way things turned out, he just felt cheated."

"I've had a witness tell me that she thought he was doing some illegal work for a drug dealer. Do you think that's possible?"

"I'm not some starry-eyed kid straight out of college. Yeah, I believe that's possible. Best job he had was as a bouncer. Trouble was, he just didn't have the size or the training. Kept it up until the second beating he took. If he hadn't been a convicted felon, I would have suggested to him that he go to the law enforcement academy."

He gave me some numbers for people that Rybeck had listed as references. Some of them had stood up as character witnesses at his last trial. For the moment, I decided that I'd heard enough about Rybeck. What I needed was to know what dirty work he was involved in, but I wasn't going to get that from his friends. I seemed destined for a trip up to Columbus.

I ran over to Dr. Barnhill's, where everyone was busy getting their canine and feline boarders and patients settled back into their proper place. I took pictures of all the employees, including Cara, watching their reactions. None of them hesitated or seemed unnerved that I was photographing them. I told them that we needed the photos for our investigation. I didn't give them any other explanation and none of them asked for more.

Darlene called as I was taking the last picture.

"A state trooper found Rybeck's car at a truck stop outside of Tallahassee. They've got it roped off, waiting for us. Marcus is going to follow us over there."

"I'll meet you at the office in ten minutes and we can ride together."

When we got to the truck stop, we found the Sentra parked in a back corner of the huge lot, on the side where the semis parked. The state trooper was waiting for us in his car.

"People are stupid. As soon as I saw it sitting back here, I knew I had to come check it out. If they'd parked it up where everyone else parks, I might not have noticed it," the trooper said. He was on the tall side, but his shoulders were narrow. Not physically intimidating, but he had the same steely eyes of every state trooper I'd ever met. Making dozens of traffic stops every day raises the odds of life-threatening situations.

"I guess there aren't many bad guys that have read 'The Purloined Letter,'" I said and, from his look, I guessed there weren't many state troopers who had either. "We appreciate your vigilance," I said, trying to make up for a joke that had obviously gone over his head.

"No problem. That's what we're here for. Murder case?"

I could tell from his inflexion that he wanted to hear all about it, so I gave him the Highlights-from-Hamlet version. Marcus took pictures of the car while I chatted with the trooper. Darlene was busy questioning the truck stop employees, trying to learn how long the car had been parked there and if anyone saw the driver.

"I better go help my partner," I told the trooper.

"She seems pretty tough," he said admiringly, which caused me to take another look at him as I walked away.

Darlene was already talking with the truck stop manager, who seemed happy to cooperate.

"Police, excellent," the man said to me. He was from Mumbai and the truck stop was a mom and pop and uncle and nephew and cousin operation.

"I have very, very good cameras," he told us as he led us back to the office. "I already called my son, Neel. He understands all of this technology."

When we entered the office, Neel was sitting in front of a bank of monitors.

"I've pulled up the ones that show that car. I'm afraid there isn't a very good view of the driver," Neel said.

"But these are the very best cameras," his father said, sounding shocked that they hadn't captured a perfect mugshot of the driver.

"The driver never comes near the building," Neel said. "I can't even be sure if it's a man or a woman. They're wearing a hoodie."

He pointed at the screen as the Sentra moved past one camera and disappeared behind a semi. Neel fast-forwarded the video to a point when the truck moved out of the frame. I could see the Sentra parked where the trooper had found it. The driver was gone.

"Did you look for a person in a hoodie on any of the other cameras?" Darlene asked.

"Yes. I looked, but I didn't see anyone suspicious. I can save the footage for you."

"Is that time stamp correct?" I asked Neel.

"Yes. I have it synced with the atomic clock."

Nerd, I thought. Aloud, I said, "Save us everything on all the cameras for two hours before and two hours after the car showed up." I wanted to make sure that, if someone had picked up the driver, we had a chance of seeing their car. We might not even know what type of vehicle we were looking for until we had a suspect.

"No problem. If you want, I can put it on a thumb drive," Neel said.

"Leave it for now. I'll have our guy come over and take a look, then he can decide what's the best way for us to get it." *Let Lionel earn his keep*, I thought.

Back out at Rybeck's car, Marcus was shaking his head. "Our bad guy wiped it down. No doubt about that. I haven't found anything."

"Did you find any keys?" Darlene asked.

"Not in any of the usual places. I checked the tire wells and under the back bumper. Nothing. Tow truck's on its way to take it to our yard. We'll tear it apart there."

Even though it wasn't the scene of the crime, it was a pretty safe bet that the killer had driven the car over here, so we needed to get any trace evidence that we could out of it.

The sun had already set when I pulled into my driveway. Cara had eaten and taken a bath by the time I settled down to the barbeque she'd brought home. She sat down next to me on the couch. Normally fresh and ready for anything, tonight she was obviously dragging.

"Tired?" I asked.

"Better now that I've had a bath. At least we got all the animals back in our place." She scratched Alvin, who had jumped up and settled down beside her. "Still, I think everyone realizes that one of us must have helped the victim get into the clinic, and once you go down that road, the thoughts just get darker."

"We found the guy's car. But so far there isn't anything in it or on it that's going to break the case open," I told her, resting my hand on hers.

She sighed. "Do you want the bad news first?"

"Is there any good news?"

"No, not really."

"In that case, hit me with the bad news," I told her, wondering what was coming.

"Mom and Dad are coming up."

At first I wasn't sure I'd heard her correctly. I stared at her and she just nodded.

"Okay, that'll be fine, once we get this case cleared up and have the house in order," I said, looking around at the stacked boxes and assorted household goods that we still hadn't tackled since Cara and Alvin had moved in.

"They're coming tomorrow," Cara said, wincing in advance of my reaction.

For a moment, I thought my head might explode. The unique personalities of her parents made them interesting people to be around, but it also made them intimidating house guests. I wasn't ready for that.

"They can't stay here," I said, simply stating a fact, not giving a command.

"No, they know that. They insisted that they wouldn't intrude on us. Mom was quite adamant that they won't stay in our place."

"I guess that's okay then. It's not that I don't like your parents, but with everything else going on right now…"

"You don't have to tell me. You know I love them, but living with them can be a challenge. I made the mistake of telling them about the murder. I should have known how they'd react. Dad got protective and Mom went into nurturing mode."

"I can understand their reaction. It'll be fine. We'll go to dinner with them, and you can spend as much time as you want with them. Where are they planning to stay?"

"I'm not sure. Mom just assured me it wouldn't be in our house."

"Calhoun's motel selection isn't great, but Tallahassee's not that far away." Tallahassee seemed like the perfect distance. Close enough to get together with them a couple of times for dinner, and not too far for Cara to go over whenever she wanted. "You can take them to the natural history museum."

"If I have time. We're still playing catch-up from canceling two days' worth of routine appointments. And the clinic's phone was ringing off the hook this afternoon. I think some people just want to make an appointment so they can come in and see the scene of the murder."

"Gawkers. You're probably right."

I understood the urge to gawk, but I was bothered by people who gave in to it. It wasn't any particular moral standard that kept me from gawking, but rather the superstitious belief that if I received even the tiniest thrill from someone else's tragedy, then I'd suffer a similar fate. It was all about Karma.

CHAPTER SIX

I'd just arrived at the office Friday morning when Darlene texted me that we had a meeting with John's parents in half an hour. I texted back that I was in the parking lot, even as I thought how stupid it was not to just walk into the building and let her see me for herself.

"They insisted they didn't mind coming here. I offered to meet them at their motel," Darlene said. I shrugged. It wasn't like the location of the meeting was going to make it any less unpleasant for everyone.

We were standing in the small lobby. Sergeant Dill Kirby was manning the front desk. We could have asked him to escort Rybeck's parents to the conference room, but I couldn't do that to grieving family members. The least we could do was to meet them at the door. I appreciated the fact that Darlene was as willing I was to go a little out of her way to show the family some respect.

Mr. and Mrs. Rybeck looked as beaten down as you would expect for two people who had just lost a child. Mr. Rybeck was a tall man who walked a little hunched over, hovering protectively above his much smaller wife.

Darlene and I introduced ourselves and offered our condolences.

"Can we get you anything before we sit down?" I asked. All either of them could manage was a shake of the head.

Once we were all seated, I told them as much as I could about their son's death. Both of them looked at me as if I was babbling nonsense.

"I don't understand. Was he robbed?" his father asked.

"The killer took his car, but abandoned it later, so we don't think that was the motive for his killing," I said.

"I don't mean to be harsh, but you do know that your son had been in trouble with the law on multiple occasions, right?" Darlene asked in her softest tone.

"We are well aware of our son's shortcomings regarding the law. I've spent a small fortune on lawyers over the years. But why would John break into a veterinary clinic?"

"We saw him just a month ago and he looked fine. I know that he probably did what they call 'recreational' drugs, but he wasn't an addict. I guess there are drugs that an addict might want from a vet..." Mrs. Rybeck's voice trailed off.

"Who killed him? If someone caught him trying to break into the clinic, why wouldn't they have called the police?" Mr. Rybeck put in.

"We don't think that's what happened," I told them. "Honestly, we're still trying to find the motive for the killing. When we do that, we'll be much closer to discovering *who* killed him. Right now we think it's possible that John had a connection with someone who works at the vet. I want to show you some pictures. If anyone looks familiar to you, or if you think that John talked about them, just speak up."

I'd brought a laptop into the room so that they could look at decent-sized versions of the pictures I'd taken yesterday. I pulled them up and began to scroll through them.

"This is Dr. Tom Barnhill. He owns the clinic." The Rybecks shrugged.

"Cara Laursen, a veterinary technician." Again, no reaction.

"Now we have Sandra Strom. She's the office manager."

I saw Mrs. Rybeck shake her head just a little. "What?" I asked.

She seemed startled. "I didn't mean to... I worked as an office manager for a dentist for almost ten years. Tough work. When you told us her job, it just made me think of that."

I looked at her closely, but there was no sign that she was hiding anything.

"Next is Gayle Patterson, who works as the receptionist." More blank stares.

"Terry Ward is the other vet tech," I said and saw Mr. Rybeck looking thoughtful. "Do you recognize him?"

"I don't think so. He just looks familiar somehow."

"He looks like that actor from that show you watch," his wife told him.

"What show?"

"You know, the one with the marshal in Kentucky or somewhere."

"*Justified?*"

"That's the one."

"You're right. He does look a bit like Marshal Givens," Mr. Rybeck said.

Moving on, I thought.

"This is Scott Wilkens. He cleans the kennels and walks the dogs."

"He's just a boy," Mrs. Rybeck said sadly.

"We can't rule out the possibility that anyone could be linked to your son."

"No, I don't recognize him," Mr. Rybeck said.

"Last is Angie Conner. She's also a kennel tech."

"No, nothing," Mr. Rybeck said.

I read off the list of names one more time. "So you're both sure you never heard John mention any of these people?"

Both of them shook their heads.

"All right. Thanks for taking a look. Now we want to talk about John's past."

"He hasn't lived with us for years," Mrs. Rybeck said.

"I know. But since we don't know why he was killed, we have to look at every angle," Darlene told them. "Was there anyone in his past that might have held a grudge against him?"

"That's the funny thing about John. Everybody liked him. Even people who had cause to be mad at him liked him. When he'd get into trouble at school, the teacher or the principal always spent at least five minutes telling us how much they liked John before they'd tell us what he'd done. Honestly, I think that was part of his problem. If people could have stayed mad at him, he might have realized that the stupid stuff he did was wrong." His father shook his head.

"He just wanted to help his friends. I couldn't get it into his head that the means were as important as the ends," Mrs. Rybeck added.

"One time, when he was a sophomore in high school, he broke into a man's house and stole a bunch of paperwork and computers. When they caught him, it turned out that it was the landlord of his girlfriend's family. The landlord was threatening to evict them and John got it into his head that if he stole all the evidence that the man owned the house, then he wouldn't be able to kick them out. I know it sounds stupid, but John was just a kid. He didn't even keep the computers or try to sell them. He dropped them off at Goodwill."

"He got into trouble more than once trying to help others. His uncle nicknamed him Quixote."

"Girls. Girls could talk him into anything," Mr. Rybeck sighed.

"Did he have any enemies?" I asked.

"Oh, there were a few silly things, but not anyone I'd say had a grudge against him," answered Mrs. Rybeck.

"Jealous boyfriends? Any husbands or scorned women?"

"He never kept a girlfriend for too long," his father answered.

"The bad ones used him and then kicked him to the curb, and the good ones got tired of him fooling around."

Darlene perked up. "Fooling around?"

"I don't mean like that. I mean not holding down a job or taking life seriously," Mrs. Rybeck clarified. "You know, all of his run-ins with the law... I think there was a part of him that just craved the excitement."

"Only thing he was ever serious about was the ROTC. He loved that. Being a part of it is what got him through high school."

"Several people have told us that John wanted to join the Army."

I saw a dark shadow cross Mr. Rybeck's face.

"I blame myself. He turned eighteen in January of his senior year. He wanted to sign enlistment papers that day. They would have let him finish school and everything. I should have let him. But, no, I thought he should finish high school before making the commitment. I told him that there was plenty of time. Promised him that if he graduated in June, took a couple of weeks to think about it, and then still wanted to enlist, I'd give him a down payment on a car."

"You just wanted to make sure he thought about it. He was eighteen and he didn't need your permission anyway," Mrs. Rybeck said with the weariness of someone who has made the same argument a thousand times.

"But he wouldn't do it without my blessing. That's the kind of kid he was. It was ironic. He wouldn't make a big decision like that without talking to me first, but he'd break the law for a lark. Crazy kid. Anyway, the night he graduated he was out with a couple of kids and they broke into an ice cream shop. Stupid, just stupid. He was the oldest and, even though everyone said that he had tried to talk them out of it, he was charged with a felony because the owner claimed that they'd done more than five hundred dollars in damage. The judge was an ass. And John ended up with that felony on his record, which kept him from being able to join the Army."

"He was devastated," Mrs. Rybeck added.

"And more mad at himself than at me."

"What did he do after that?" I asked.

The Rybecks told us how John spent the next few years skipping from town to town. Each time, he'd seem to be getting his act together and maturing and then he would do something stupid. Usually he'd find a way to get in trouble with the law. He'd go to court, do his penance and move on.

"When did he move to Columbus?"

"Three years ago, maybe four," Mr. Rybeck said, looking at his wife for confirmation.

"Closer to four. I think he liked being near the Army base."

"That's right, he always talked about hanging out with the soldiers from the base."

"Did he mention anyone specific that he hung out with?" Darlene asked.

"No. Though he talked about an old guy who lived next door. A Vietnam veteran. I can't remember his name. Let's see… Can you think of anyone else?" he asked his wife.

You could tell that the two of them were used to working together. Rybeck may have had problems, but he didn't lack for loving parents.

"He mentioned a couple of girls. Just one at a time, of course. But I'm afraid I never took him too seriously. I always figured that one day he'd bring a girl home and that would be the one I'd need to remember," Mrs. Rybeck said regretfully.

"Did you notice anything different about John since he'd been living in Columbus?" I asked and saw husband and wife exchange significant looks. "Anything you can tell me might help us find his killer."

Mr. Rybeck sighed heavily. "There was one thing that we'd both noticed… I know what you're going to think. I guess we thought it too. But…"

"You need to tell us whatever you can," Darlene urged.

"Go on, tell them," Mrs. Rybeck, said putting her hand on his.

"I don't know that anything was wrong, but he wasn't asking us for money. It's been over a year since he asked us for help. In the past, he'd never gone more than a couple of months without needing help paying some bill or another. He'd find work, and he'd work hard, but he always ended up getting bored or screwing up some way. John changed jobs as frequently as most people get a haircut. Because of that, he went without a paycheck more often than not."

"He never needed much," his mother said.

"Usually just a couple hundred dollars. He never would have asked if he thought we were in need. It was just getting-by cash. We've had friends whose kids got into drugs and they were always begging for money. John wasn't like that."

"And the poor Martins. Their girl was an awful gambler," Mrs. Rybeck reminded her husband. "That girl bled them dry, even forged their names and took out a mortgage on their house."

He nodded. "With John it was just a phone bill, the electric bill, or money for a deposit on an apartment. That kind of thing."

"But lately he'd had money?" I asked.

"Seemed to. At first I felt pretty good about him showing some financial independence, but when I'd ask him about his work, he'd just say he was doing this and that. Never a straight answer, which wasn't like him. Normally, every new job he got was the best ever for the first month or so and he wouldn't stop talking about it."

"We know what you must think," Mrs. Rybeck said. "And maybe he *was* doing something illegal. But you've got to understand, if he was, then it didn't involve hurting anyone."

"Do you think he would sell drugs, or maybe help transport them?" I asked.

The Rybecks shared a glance. "He might. I wish I could say no, but I think he might see something like running drugs as an adventure," his father said.

I made a mental note to call Eddie Thompson, the

confidential informant that I used whenever the question of drugs came up. If Rybeck was connected with the local drug culture, then Eddie might know about it.

"You even said something to him about that," Mrs. Rybeck pointed out.

"I did. Once I realized that he had money and a job that he didn't want to talk about, I told him he had to be careful. Get hooked up with the wrong people and you might not be able to get out, I said."

"What was his response?"

"Told me not to worry. Said he was learning to take care of himself. I thought that was kind of odd at the time. Guess it was stupid of me not to follow up on it," Mr. Rybeck said.

"Funny thing was, he seemed happier than we'd seen him in a long time," Mrs. Rybeck told us.

"Probably why I didn't press him."

"Guess you were happy that he was making his own money," Darlene said nonjudgmentally.

"Sure, though money never mattered much to him. You say you found his car, so you can see that he wasn't a big spender. There was nothing flashy about him. If he had money, he spent it. Buy drinks for other people or loan cash to his friends. That's the kind of thing he liked to do with his money."

They sounded so sure. I'd learned over the years to take anything a parent said with a hundred-pound grain of salt, but these two didn't strike me as the type that would fool themselves.

We asked a dozen more questions and answered a few of theirs, then let them go. We walked them out to their car and both Darlene and I gave them our cards and cell numbers.

"Call us anytime," Darlene said.

"We'll do our best to keep you informed on the status of the investigation. You have my word that we'll do everything we can to catch your son's killer," I added.

"Thank you, but there isn't any justice that will help us," Mr. Rybeck said before turning and getting stiffly into the driver's seat.

Darlene and I looked at each other grimly as he drove away. He was right, but the least we could do was to make the murderer pay the price for what they had done.

CHAPTER SEVEN

"So, by all accounts, John Rybeck was the male equivalent of the prostitute with the heart of gold," I said as we walked back into the building.

"Hard to believe, but…" Darlene shrugged. I could tell that the Rybecks had swayed her too.

"So far we haven't heard a harsh word about him."

"Could he have gotten into trouble playing do-gooder?"

"He certainly sounds like the type."

We'd both seen it. Anyone who's been in law enforcement for at least a year or so will have their stories of the guy who thinks he's a junior cop and goes around trying to make citizen arrests. As a rule, these guys are a pain in the ass, and sometimes they get their own selves into trouble, either with the law or with the bad guys.

"Of course, as you know all too well, the cop wannabe can turn out to be a serial killer himself," Darlene said and my hand went unconsciously to the scar on my left side. You didn't have to delve too deeply into the ranks of serial rapists and murderers to find the ones that used fake badges or an interest in police work as part of their MO.

"And sometimes the wannabe really is just a good guy trying to do the right thing and it still breaks bad for him.

Look at the guy in the Atlanta Olympic bombing."

"Richard Jewell. He did the right thing, saved lives, and he was still accused of being the bad guy."

"So maybe we have a Richard Jewell here," I suggested.

"Which leaves us with the question of what he was doing in the clinic that night."

"And the answer to that can probably be found at Dr. Barnhill's. So do we question his staff there or here?" I asked, inclining my head toward the conference room.

"Is it better to question them where they're relaxed, or to put them under a little pressure here?"

The answer depended on whether we thought they intended to cooperate, in which case we'd want them to be relaxed. On the other hand, if we thought there was a chance someone would be hostile, then we'd want to put some pressure on them right from the start, since we were going to have to sweat it out of them anyway.

"One of them is hiding something. Whether that someone is directly involved in the killing or just made some bad decisions, they had a chance to fess up the first time we talked with them. I say we bring them here," I said.

"Agreed."

I pulled out my phone and called the clinic. I told Dr. Barnhill that we needed to speak with all of his employees, but that we'd leave it to them to decide in what order they wanted to come to our office. He told me that he'd have Sandra work out the details with the staff.

"Is Gayle back in the office?"

"Yes, she was here first thing this morning. She was very upset. She said a relative texted her when the news broke," Dr. Barnhill told me.

I wasn't surprised. We were lucky if we could keep an investigation quiet for ten minutes these days, let alone a couple of days. I didn't tell him that we had planned to put out a pick-up order on Gayle if she hadn't shown up at work. People who changed their routines or disappeared shortly before or after a murder put themselves smack dab in the crosshairs.

"Please see that she is at the top of the list," I said, being polite but firm.

While we waited for Barnhill's staff to sort out their schedules, we enjoyed a potluck lunch in the staff room to celebrate Major Sam Parks' birthday. The table was laden with a dozen samples of comfort food and a truly sinful cake made by Beth Miller, our head records clerk. Seriously, she must have used a whole bag of sugar and a tub of butter to make the thing. After joining in on a lot of good-natured ribbing at the expense of Parks, who acted as sheriff when Dad was out of pocket, Darlene and I made our way back to our desks.

Gayle arrived soon after and we took her into the small conference room. I had seen her dozens of times at the clinic, but now I was looking at her through the lens of a murder investigation. She was maybe 5'5" with long brown hair in a braid down her back. Her eyes were soft, the lids a bit droopy. She was wearing the only type of clothes I had ever seen her in—colorful scrubs with a cute animal print on them. Her only jewelry was a gold chain with her name and a shamrock hanging from it. I could see now why Cara thought she was rather plain and not necessarily the type to catch the eye of a good-looking guy. I would be curious to meet the Mr. Dawson.

Once we were seated, we turned on the recorder and had Gayle confirm her name, address and willingness to be interviewed. Then Darlene started with the questions.

"Where were you on Tuesday night?"

"My boyfriend and I went to Atlanta for a couple days. He had a meeting up there. I asked Dr. Barnhill for permission. We left Tuesday afternoon. I came in early and opened up so I could get off early. Normally, I don't do any of the kennel work, but I did on Tuesday since Wayne asked me to go with him and we wanted to leave in the early afternoon so we could get up there before too late. The hotel was really nice. We had a room overlooking the pool and—"

I held up my hand to stop her. She rambled on more like a teenager than a woman of forty. "When exactly did you leave town?" I asked, hoping to get her back on track.

"I guess we got on the road about three-thirty after we went by my place and picked up my suitcases. I had to pack a lot because I wanted some clothes for lounging around the pool and we were going out to dinner Wednesday night. Wayne took me to a really, really nice place. Very expensive. So naturally I had to have dressy clothes, and—" I made the traffic cop motion again.

"What time did you check in to the hotel?" I asked, wondering how much she could say in answer to a simple question like that.

"We got there about nine o'clock because we hit some traffic going through all the small, dinky towns north of here. We made pretty good time once we got on the interstate at Tifton, but I was hungry, so when we got to Macon we stopped at a Cracker Barrel. I got the country fried steak and Wayne got—"

My hand shot up again. I wanted to ask her why on earth she thought we would be interested in what Wayne had to eat, but I was afraid that she'd be more than happy to tell me. How the hell Wayne had managed to stay in the car with this woman all the way up to and back from Atlanta was beyond me. I was even more interested in getting to meet Wayne. I didn't know how he could be connected to our murder, but I found it hard to believe that an average person would find Gayle irresistible.

"Try and be as concise as possible. Now, when did you learn of the murder at the clinic?"

"Oh my gawd!" she said, putting her hand up to her mouth as if she was hearing about the murder for the first time. "Can you believe it? Of course you can. You're cops and that's why you're asking me all of these questions. But I couldn't believe it. Aunt Millie texted me, I guess it was about noon on Wednesday. I was flabbergasted. I told Wayne and he couldn't believe it either. Murder. Someone murdered right there in the clinic not forty feet from where I work every day. It's crazy! And someone I'd never heard of. Of course, thank the good lord that it wasn't someone I knew. How much worse would that be?"

"That's fine. Noon on Wednesday. A text from your Aunt Millie. Could I have a look at the text?" I asked, holding out my hand. Gayle took her phone out of her big, flowered handbag and handed it to me.

"Would you like to pull up the text?" I asked, holding the phone out toward her.

"No, you're fine. Just go to my messages and look for Auntie M. We chat back and forth all the time so it's right there at the top. She's just been burning it up since the murder too. I think she likes all the excitement. I told her, 'shame on you,' I said. 'You shouldn't be getting any entertainment out of other people's troubles.' But I was just kidding her. She's the sweetest person you'd ever want to meet, and she would absolutely die if she thought she was doing anything improper…"

I tuned her out as I scanned through her messages. I took a quick glance at the texts between her and Wayne while I had the chance, since she apparently didn't care, but didn't see anything that stood out. I found the text in question from Auntie M and it was as described. I'd had to skim through dozens upon dozens of texts between them before I found it. Gayle had not exaggerated about Auntie M's excitement over the crime. I hoped the investigation would not require me to be in close contact with her. Right there and then I decided that, if the aunt needed to be questioned, I'd figure out some way to trick Darlene into doing it.

We showed Gayle a picture of John Rybeck and asked if she recognized him. After a ten-minute ramble about how poor she was at recognizing faces, we got a tentative no. She told us that she'd never been to Columbus or Phenix City and didn't know anyone up there, though she managed to mention half a dozen people who, as far as I could tell, didn't live anywhere near Columbus and had nothing whatsoever to do with any of the questions we had asked her.

After getting contact information for Wayne, we pushed Gayle out the door. I enjoyed a moment of blessed silence before I turned to Darlene and said, "I think we can rest assured that she's not the mastermind behind this, but she wouldn't be that hard to manipulate."

"Does make me want to meet Wayne," Darlene said, rolling her eyes a bit.

The next employee to show up for questioning was Terry Ward. I'd spent a bit of time around Terry as he was one of Cara's good friends as well as a co-worker. He was nice and soft-spoken. He had some odd opinions about food and health, but that seemed to be the norm these days. I'd met his long-term partner, Rick, on two occasions, and I liked them both.

I looked at Terry closely as he walked toward us. After the Rybecks had pointed out that he looked like Timothy Olyphant, I couldn't get it out of my head. I could see the resemblance in his eyes and the shape of his face and mouth—not a perfect match, but there were definitely similarities.

"Hey, Terry," I greeted him, shaking his hand. "How's the wedding planning coming?"

"Argggh! Don't even get me started. Why do caterers have to charge so much extra for good food? If we wanted to serve greasy garbage, it would be half the price… Like I said, don't get me started. Sorry—I'm rambling. The murder has me more than a little shaken up."

"Don't worry. We just spent an hour with Gayle," I said with a grin.

"That woman loves to hear herself talk. I shouldn't make fun. She really is sweet."

"We'll start with the basics. Where were you on Tuesday night?"

"Rick and I spent the night binge-watching *House of Cards*. We stayed up until one-thirty."

This gave him very little alibi since their house was less than a mile from the clinic. "You live just north of the square?" I asked, confirming this.

"Yes. It's Rick's house, really. He's… Well, you know he teaches at the university in Tallahassee, but he likes living in a small town. It's a Craftsman, built in the '20s, and we're working at restoring it." He paused for a minute, then said, "Look, I've watched my share of detective shows, so I know what you're thinking. Yes, I walk to work most days. I could have gone over there anytime that night, probably without Rick even knowing. But I didn't."

"Have you ever been to Phenix City, Alabama?" Darlene asked.

"I don't even know where that is."

"How about Columbus, Georgia?"

"Sure, I've been there. Rick and I went up to Callaway Gardens two years ago for the Fantasy in Lights and we drove through Columbus."

"Phenix City is just over the river from Columbus."

"I see. No, we just drove through Columbus."

I showed him a copy of John Rybeck's driver's license photo and asked if he recognized him.

Terry took his time. "Is this the man that was murdered?"

"Yes."

"I think I *have* seen him," Terry said. His hand shook a little as he held the picture.

"Where?"

"Not far from the clinic. It was the other morning when I was walking to work. I passed a car and… I can't be one hundred percent sure. You know, you hate to stare at someone, but it was really unusual to see someone parked on the side of the road at that hour."

"What type of car was it?"

"I'm not a car guy. Just an ordinary car, light colored…" He scrunched up his face in thought. "It wasn't new. I thought it was dirty."

I pulled up a picture of Rybeck's car that I had on my phone and showed it to him. "Does this look like the car?"

"Yes, I think so."

"When exactly was this?" Darlene asked.

"Monday morning."

"Could you show us where you saw the car?"

"Yes. Well, pretty close, at least."

I looked over at Darlene and she nodded, standing up. "Come on. We'll run up there now and take a look," I said.

"Do you think it's important?" he asked, a little surprised by our eagerness. He had no way of knowing that we had very few leads. Knowing where the victim was a day and a half before the murder couldn't hurt.

"At this point, everything has the potential to be important," I answered.

We drove the mile or so in my car. When we were a block away from Barnhill's clinic, we got out and walked. Just in case we found something interesting, I brought along my pack that included evidence bags and gloves.

The spot Terry showed us was nicely placed to give someone sitting in a car a good view of the back of the clinic, where there was a quarter acre of fenced-in space for exercising dogs.

"He had a good view and this tree and bushes would provide him with some cover," I observed.

"Still, someone coming out the back door would be able to see a car parked here," Darlene pointed out.

"What did the man appear to be doing?" I asked Terry, who looked very uncomfortable.

"Just looking at his phone. I figured he was texting or posting something," Terry answered, looking everywhere but at us.

"What's wrong?" I asked him.

He looked at me. "I've just been thinking that maybe I should have said something. I knew that a car shouldn't have been here at that hour. I just figured he was parked to text or was waiting for somebody. If it had been late at night, I might have thought that he was up to no good, but who thinks like that at seven in the morning?" Terry was clearly frustrated at a world that didn't work the way he thought it should.

"You can't blame yourself. Most of the time it's true. You can walk through the worst parts of most cities at nine in the morning because the bad guys are still asleep. Besides, this was the victim you saw, not the bad guy."

"But he broke into the clinic," Terry said hesitantly.

"Maybe not. If he was parked here and saw someone go into the clinic late at night, he might have been being a Good Samaritan. Maybe he went to see what was up and got himself killed in the process," I told him.

Darlene finished questioning Terry while I walked up and down the street, looking in the gutter and under bushes, picking up items that might mean something, though it was hard to imagine what. But if we found a suspect who claimed never to have met John, and we could prove that both of their DNA was on the same object, then we'd have some solid evidence that the suspect was lying. All of it was a long shot, but most of the time we had to put our money down on the long shots.

When I took my collection of what was most likely trash back to the car, Terry said he'd walk back to the clinic.

"What about your car? Didn't you drive to our office?"

"No, Cara dropped me off. She was headed out to meet her parents."

I pulled out my phone and looked at it. I'd had the alerts turned off and, sure enough, there was a text from Cara reporting that her parents had called and she was going to meet them at our place. *Our place? That sounds ominous*, I thought.

CHAPTER EIGHT

Our next interview was with Scott Wilkins, one of the kennel techs. He was just nineteen, with a large build and a big round face that was always smiling.

"Your family owns a farm on the west side of the county, right?" I asked.

"That's right. We've farmed it for, like, a hundred years," he said. *More than that*, I thought, knowing that his was one of the first families to settle in Adams County back in the 1840s.

"You like working for Dr. Barnhill?"

"I do. It's different than the farm. Lot cooler in the summer. I'm taking some classes at Florida A&M too."

After the preliminaries, Darlene got down to business. "Scott, have you ever seen this man before?" she asked, showing him the picture of John Rybeck.

"He's the guy that got killed? No, I don't think so," he said hesitantly.

"What about this car? Have you seen it parked near the clinic?"

"I don't know. It looks pretty much like every other car." He shrugged.

"Have you noticed anything odd or different at the clinic

over the last couple of weeks?"

"You don't think anyone there had anything to do with killing this guy, do you? Didn't he just break in and then—" He broke off, seeming to realize that the burglary scenario didn't lead anywhere. What burglar breaks into a clinic and then stabs himself with a syringe filled with animal tranquilizer? Even if there was the slightest chance that this was a suicide, it still didn't explain how he got in and who turned off the alarm and the surveillance cameras.

"You see our problem. Someone killed him."

"So he didn't really break in, did he?"

"There weren't any signs of a forced entry."

"Someone helped him. That's crazy." Scott seemed genuinely upset by the idea. "But everybody's so nice."

I could see that he was really pretty unworldly. I wondered how hard it would have been for someone to manipulate him.

"People aren't always what they seem to be," I said. "Has anyone asked you to do anything odd at the clinic?"

"Like what?"

"Like leave a door unlocked or to hand over the clinic's key. You have a key for when you take care of the dogs in the morning, right?"

"Yeah, I'm on every other weekend. I come in and walk all the dogs, clean out the crates and the dog runs."

"And you're by yourself on Sundays?"

"Yeah, on my Sundays it's just me. I work until about noon, go home and then come back for feeding time around six and walk everyone again. If there's something wrong with one of the animals, I'll call Cara or Terry. Sometimes they'll tell me to go ahead and call Dr. Barnhill."

"Do you leave the doors unlocked when you work?" I asked. A thought had occurred to me. I'd been there a few times when Cara was helping with some of the kennel duties and the barking was so loud that anyone could have come into the clinic without her knowing it. I'd actually pointed this out to her and asked her to be extra careful and to make sure the doors were locked if she was there alone.

"Never the front door. But if I'm coming and going out the back walking dogs, then I just leave that door unlocked. I never prop it open, though. I did that once the first couple of weeks I worked there, and when I was cleaning out one of the cat's crates he got loose and ran outside. I was scared to death that I wasn't going to be able to catch him. Luckily, it was Samson and he was easy. Some of the other cats, I'd have never seen them again."

"It's pretty loud when you're cleaning out the dog runs, isn't it?"

"I wear my earbuds and listen to music," he said and I didn't have to ask if he would hear anyone coming in. The answer was obvious.

"Where were you on Tuesday night?" Darlene asked.

"My brother and I went up to an equipment auction in Georgia."

"What time did you get back?"

"Around two o'clock."

"You ever been to Columbus or Phenix City?"

"Been to Fort Benning. My cousin was stationed there. He showed us the tanks they drive. Pretty cool."

"Is he still stationed there?"

"No, that was last year. He's over in Savannah now."

It was a connection. A tenuous one, but still a connection. It was theoretically possible that his cousin had known John Rybeck. We got his name and the bit of contact information that Scott was able to provide.

Sandra Strom, the office manager, arrived a few minutes after Scott left. Sandra was dressed for her job in a clinic polo and khaki pants. I knew that she was close to forty, but she could have easily passed for thirty. She wore cat earrings that were partly hidden by her blonde hair. I'd met her several times and she had always appeared composed and in control. Today, as we greeted her, she just looked sad.

"This is such an awful business. What do you think he was looking for?" she asked.

"We're still trying to figure that out ourselves," I told her.

"I hate to sound callous, but my first thought was a fear that this might hurt the clinic. However, the people around here seem to have a rather ghoulish fascination with the murder."

"I think you'll find that most people have a little ghoul in them," Darlene said. "Where are you from originally?"

"Oh, I'm from New Orleans. I was born and raised there. My folks lived in the Irish Channel. They call it the Irish Channel, but the truth is there were some of us Germans there too. Dad worked on the docks. He said you couldn't go wrong if you lived in a neighborhood where people worked with their hands. Of course, now it's full of college students and who knows who else."

"Your parents still live there?"

"No. Mom passed away a couple of years ago and Dad lives on the other side of Lake Pontchartrain. He couldn't stand being in the house after Mom died."

"What brought you to Adams County?"

"The job. I was working as an office manager in Macon for a medical supply company. But the owner died and when the son took over, he was just running it into the ground. So I started checking out the job listings. Dr. Barnhill was looking for someone, so I came down here and we hit it off. It's been about three years now. Happy endings all around."

Was there something hiding behind her smile? Surely Dr. Barnhill wasn't able to pay her as much as a medical supply company. But, of course, work is work. If the company you're working for is going under, a nice veterinary clinic might sound like a pleasant change. When was the last time a vet went out of business?

We showed her the pictures of John and his car and got headshakes.

"I've never seen the poor man. I can't imagine how this could have happened. I'd told Dr. Barnhill that we should be more careful about tracking the office keys, but he seemed to think that, as long as the drugs were locked in the safe, then we were okay. I even explained to him that there are crack addicts that'll rip the copper wiring right out of the walls. People will break in and steal anything these days. At any rate, I did insist that all of our computer records be backed up daily through a secure service."

"Have you noticed anyone acting strangely in the last couple of weeks?" I asked her.

She pursed her lips and tilted her head in thought. "Gayle hasn't stopped talking about her new boyfriend. Not that she ever stops talking, boyfriend or not. I swear, he must need earplugs to be around her. I don't mean to be catty. She's always been talkative, but now with Wayne to talk about, she is just non-stop. Other than that, I don't know. Of course, Cara has been excited about moving in with you, Larry. She is so happy. I'm so glad for you two. Pretty much everything else has been normal."

She paused for a moment and then her mouth dropped open. "You think this involves one of us! What a wicked thought. I just can't imagine that. I know we've been pretty lax about our security, but are you sure that one of us is involved?"

"No, not at all," I assured her. "It just seems to be the most likely explanation. But, as you said, we're also looking at your security, or the lack thereof."

"We had a man out this morning to change all of the locks, and we're instituting some new protocols."

"Glad to hear it. I discussed that with Dr. Barnhill yesterday," Darlene said.

"Where were you Tuesday night?" I asked.

"I was home alone. I watched TV for a few hours and then went to bed. Jeez, it's so hard not to make some stupid joke about how, if I'd known someone was going to be murdered, I'd have had a better alibi. The whole thing is just crazy."

"Where do you live?"

"I rent a house in Oak Ridge. Deputy Henley lives not too far from me. I've met him at a couple of neighborhood events. It's nice living in a family-oriented subdivision."

I added talking to her neighbors about her comings and goings to my list. The houses were pretty close to each other in that neighborhood and maybe someone would remember if she had left the house on Tuesday night.

"Have you ever been to Phenix City, Alabama or Columbus, Georgia?"

"Let me think. I did go over to Callaway Gardens from Macon once, but we never went into Columbus."

"Do you know anyone stationed at Fort Benning?"

"No."

We asked a few more questions, then Sandra threw one at us. "Do you think we're in any danger at the clinic?" Her brow was furrowed in concern.

"That's hard to say since we don't know why John Rybeck was murdered. But I don't think there is too much risk. You know I wouldn't let Cara be there if I thought there was. However, if one of you knows something or saw something, that could be a threat to the killer. If there's anything you know, or think you know—anything at all—then it would be important to tell us."

"Of course. I would never hold anything back from you," she said. For a moment I thought that her eyes were staring a little too hard into mine, almost as if she was trying to convince me that she was telling the truth.

CHAPTER NINE

Next was Angie Conner, the other kennel tech. She was twenty, sassy and tough. Cara often talked about how hard Angie worked.

"Kennel tech? Heh, I'm really just a pooper scooper," she said with a smile when we started off asking about her job. "But I really like helping the animals. And I'm taking classes off and on at Florida State. My problem is I don't know what I want to do. My dad told me to take my time, work some and see if anything calls to me. Dad's pretty easygoing. Mom told me to hurry up and pick something that I could find work in and that paid a decent salary. I'm trying to balance the two."

"Are you from here?"

"Crawfordville," she said, mentioning a town just south of Tallahassee. "Mom and Dad both work for the state in Tallahassee."

"Why'd you move over here?"

"Do I have to say?" she asked with a bit of a frown.

"No, but if you don't…" I let her imagination fill in the gaps regarding the risks of withholding information.

"No problem. The story just doesn't make me look very good. I met a guy. How many sad stories start that way?"

She gave a self-deprecating laugh. "He talked me into moving in with him. He was an ass, so I kicked him out."

"That's a pretty neat trick. You move in with a guy and then kick him out."

"It was a roommate situation. The guy who split the rent with him was tired of his bullshit too, so we kinda organized a coup. He was out and I was in. I'd been paying the rent for a couple of months anyway."

"What's this ex-boyfriend's name?"

"Jack Pershing."

"Was he mad that you kicked him out?"

"What do you think? We almost had to call the cops a couple of times, but he really didn't want that. He'd gotten into trouble a couple of times before and was afraid of the cops. Whenever we'd had enough and said we were going to call the cops, he'd be all apologetic and back off."

"How long ago did all of this take place?" Darlene asked.

"Right before I got the job at the vet. A year and a half."

"Where is Jack now?"

"He's around. Lives in Tallahassee. I've seen him at bars and concerts and stuff."

"When was the last time you saw him?" I asked. Here was a jerk with a grudge—always a good place to start a suspect list.

"A week ago, maybe. At a bar on Tennessee Street. He was hanging out with a girl and a couple of guys. Seriously, they all looked like meth-heads."

"Did you all speak?"

"Wait a minute. You don't seriously think he could have something to do with the murder? If so, then I've given you the wrong idea. He's an idiot, but I don't think he's dangerous. Maybe to himself."

"Let us be the judge of that. Did you speak to him?"

"No. I didn't speak to him. I'm not even sure he saw me. Like I said, all four of them looked like they were on a meth buzz."

"Have you ever seen this man?" I showed her the picture

of John Rybeck.

"I don't think so," she said with a shake of her head.

"What about this car?"

I could tell from her expression that she had expected to see another picture of someone or something that she didn't recognize. But when she saw the car, her eyes grew wide.

"I think I have," she said slowly. "It was pretty far away, but I noticed it because I'd never seen a car parked there before."

"Where was it?"

"I was watching a couple of the dogs get some exercise in the fenced-in area behind the clinic. That car was parked on the next street over. It was there for quite a while on Monday." It was the same place that Terry had pointed out.

"Did you see who was in the car?"

"No. I mean, I could see that someone was in the front, but it was too far away to get a good look."

"Did anyone else go near the car?" I asked.

"Not that I noticed."

"When exactly did you see the vehicle?"

"In the morning. I noticed it parked there when I brought out several of the dogs. That's why it sticks in my mind. Maybe from eight to possibly ten. You think that was the killer?"

"No," I said, leaving it at that.

"Did anyone else from the clinic notice the car?" Darlene asked.

"Not that I know of."

"Did you mention the car to anyone?"

"I might have. I thought it was pretty weird. My mom's all about this situational awareness thing. I think I did say something to Gayle or Sandra. Maybe even to Cara. But when we're busy, we really don't pay attention to anything that's not directly related to a client or one of the animals. Also, I think with Gayle running her mouth the way she does, a lot of us have learned to shut each other out. You forget that it's not Gayle who's talking."

Angie hadn't been to Columbus or Phenix City and didn't know anyone who lived or worked there. We finished up with our questions for her and sent her on her way with the gift of our cards and phone numbers. My watch said that it was just shy of five o'clock.

"We could do Dr. Barnhill now, since he can't easily get away during business hours, and then call it a day," I suggested.

"That would leave Cara and Mrs. Barnhill for tomorrow," Darlene said. Even though tomorrow was Saturday, I was on board with plowing ahead with the investigation. I didn't like the idea of Cara working at a place where a murder had happened with the killer still on the loose.

"That works for me. Hey, let's also hit up Gayle's boyfriend tomorrow. There's got be something fishy there."

I called the clinic and Dr. Barnhill said he'd be over as soon as he finished up with his last patient. Then I texted Cara to tell her I was going to be a little late. Her response was a succinct: *Okay*. Not her usual style, but I figured that her parents must have been keeping her busy. I hoped they'd be gone to their motel by the time I got home. I knew I was going to be too tired for a lot of socializing.

When Dr. Barnhill came into our conference room, he looked as if he had aged ten years in two days. He was still wearing his white coat.

"Long day," he told us. "We're still working to catch up. But here I am. How can I help?"

I knew Dr. Barnhill's history pretty well, so I started with the meatier questions.

"Where were you Tuesday night?"

"It's like an old detective novel. Bridget and I went to dinner in Tallahassee, then came home. We got in around ten o'clock. We both read for a while and then went to bed."

"Have you noticed anything odd at the clinic lately? Anyone acting out of the ordinary?"

"Not that I could tell. But Bridget makes fun of the fact

that I have tunnel vision. When I'm working with my patients, I don't notice much else. Office politics have always… irritated me. Maybe that's too harsh. I just don't like some of the silly stuff that the staff can get up to, so I tend to ignore it. A couple of times that's come back to bite me."

"How's that?" Darlene asked.

"Oh, well, once I didn't notice when two of my staff were having a little too much… fun together. Which was a problem since they were both married to other people. One day the wife of the man came in and pretty much trashed the reception area and both of the employees' cars with a baseball bat. Afterward, everyone told me I should have seen it coming. I don't understand why people can't leave their personal lives at home for just eight hours a day." He shook his head in frustration.

"Have you seen this man before?" I produced the picture of John Rybeck.

"That's the man that was killed, right?" He stared hard at the picture. "No, can't say that I have." The image of the car didn't ring any bells with him either.

"Have you ever been to Columbus, Georgia or Phenix City, Alabama?"

"Quite a few times. I have a sister who lives in Huntsville, and when Bridget and I want to go take the scenic route, Phenix City is on the way. We never stop there, though. It's too early in the trip."

"Know anyone stationed at Fort Benning?"

"Years ago, I had a buddy in the Army. I think he was there for a little while, but I never visited."

"How did Sandra come to work for you?"

"My wife was my office manager. She'd been doing that for almost twenty-five years. But Bridget's back and knees started bothering her a few years ago. Finally we just decided that we could afford to hire someone to do the job. We put out the word both locally and on the Internet. I guess we ended up interviewing almost a dozen people. Sandra seemed the best fit for the job."

"I'm assuming you checked her references thoroughly?"

"Yes, I called them. And she's never given me any reason to regret hiring her. I know I should have done a better job with the clinic's security. In fact, Sandra has told me that a couple of times. I just didn't think. Who would? But I can assure you, I got the locksmith to change and upgrade all of our locks today. We've also locked the computer that controls the security cameras up in its own area. So I've closed the barn door firmly now that the cows are all out." He paused. "I guess that's not a very funny joke, considering."

We ran down the rest of the employees, but he reported no problems or suspicions. After a few more questions, we finished up with promises to keep in close contact. We needed to know what was going on at the clinic, and he naturally wanted to be kept informed on how the investigation was going.

"Is there any danger to the staff?" he asked us as we walked him to the door.

"We can't be sure, of course, since we don't know the killer's motive. I doubt the killer will attack any of the staff now, but I *am* glad that you've upgraded the security." We shook hands at the door.

The sun was low in the sky and my watch said it was almost seven. Darlene and I headed back to our desks to make a few notes before leaving. I sent Cara one more text telling her that I would be home shortly.

Her response: *Looking forward to seeing you. Sorry. Prepare yourself.*

I shot back: *Why?*

Her: *You'll have to see it. Sorry.*

This left me puzzled and more than a little concerned. I thought about calling, but since I'd be home in fifteen minutes, I hurried to my car instead.

The sun was below the horizon when I came up my

driveway, leaving just enough light to see by. But what I saw made no sense. Something huge stood beside my old doublewide under the spreading live oaks. The light wasn't quite good enough to make out the details, but it appeared to be the world's biggest teepee.

By the time I'd parked and gotten out of the car, Cara was standing beside me.

"What the hell is that?" I asked her quietly, trying to keep my voice under control.

"A yurt," Cara said, barely able to meet my eyes. Looking a little shell-shocked, she opened her mouth to say more, but before she could, her mother came out of the yurt and bustled over to us.

"There you are!" Anna Laursen said warmly, gripping me in a hug. "It's so good to see you again. We are so happy that you all are living together. We were planning on visiting after Cara'd had a chance to settle in, but with the murder I told Henry that you all would need some emotional support."

"You're going to stay in the... yurt?" I asked, trying to wrap my head around the concept.

"Of course! We wouldn't dream of imposing on you. I know when Henry and I started living together, we were making love every night. Well, honestly, some nights we were just having sex." As my mind cringed at that image, she laughed loud enough that I was pretty sure my neighbors would have heard it and none of them lived closer than a quarter of a mile away.

"Anna! Where are the fire irons?" came a soft roar from the other side of the yurt.

"He's building a fire," Anna explained to me. "Larry's home!" she shouted toward the yurt. Moments later, a man who should have been followed by a blue ox came around the tent toward us.

"Larry, good to see you!" He grabbed my right hand with both of his in a grip that made me claustrophobic.

"I'm doing okay, Mr. Laursen," I answered, desperately wanting to have control of my hand back.

"Henry. Since you pulled my chestnuts out of the fire back in December, I think you can call me Henry," he said with a huge grin, still not releasing my hand.

"I was glad to do it… Henry." As if that had been the magic word, my hand was finally given back to me.

"Where's the big guy?" Henry asked in a voice that redefined booming.

"Mauser belongs to Larry's dad," Cara reminded him.

"Well, I want to see him before we leave. But there's plenty of time."

Plenty of time? I thought. *What the hell does that mean?*

"If you all will excuse us for a minute," I said to Cara's parents, starting toward the house and measuring the distance in my head. When would I be far enough away to become hysterical without hurting their feelings?

"Seriously, Cara, what the hell?" I asked when we were safely inside.

"Larry, I'm sorry. I couldn't stop them."

I knew that this was literally true. Her parents were a force of nature.

"But… couldn't you… I mean… Arrgh! I can't do this right now. I need to have a little downtime to think. I can't work this case all day and then spend the evening with your parents." I knew that my tone was coming across as accusatory, but I couldn't help feeling overwhelmed.

"I don't know what to say. At least they aren't in the house," Cara said weakly, sounding hurt.

"I guess I'll just have to deal with it," I snapped, knowing as I said it that it was harsh and unfair. I turned back to the door. "We better go talk to them."

"Larry…"

"I know. It's not your fault. I just wasn't expecting this and I'm having a bit of a hard time dealing with it." I managed to give her a look that was absent of all the irritation I was feeling. Cara reached out and I squeezed her hand.

Back outside, I helped Henry collect wood and feed the

fire that he had expertly built.

"I'll be honest, Larry. If Cara didn't have you to look into this murder, I'd have to do something about it myself."

Still feeling imposed upon, I had to bite my tongue to keep from pointing out that the last time he had become involved with a murder he had almost found himself living in Raiford courtesy of the state.

"Tell me that there is no danger to Cara working there."

"I can't give you the details, but the murder seems to have more to do with the victim than where the victim was killed. But—and this is a big but—we really don't know much right now."

"But you don't think the killer will hurt anyone at the clinic again," he said, picking up a piece of wood that probably weighed forty pounds with one hand. His ancestors must have come in very handy on those Viking raids.

"Again, all I can say is that I'd be very surprised if—" That's when my phone rang with a call from Pete. I held a finger up to Henry. "Sorry, I need to take this."

"I just got called in. I'm thinking this is one for you," Pete said.

"What have you got?"

"There's a dead body in the clinic's parking lot."

"Shit! Okay, I'll be right there."

When I told Cara that something else had happened at the clinic, she wanted to come with me, but I told her to stay with her parents. I assured her that I would call or text as soon as I could, gave her a quick kiss and headed out to the latest nightmare.

CHAPTER TEN

Red and blue lights were reflecting off of every building in the area as I drove up to the clinic. Deputy Matti Sanderson was directing traffic and pointed me to where Pete stood talking with an older couple.

When Pete saw me get out of my car, he left the couple and walked over. Behind him I could see that the whole parking lot was marked off. A dark shape was lying on the ground near a hedge at the corner of the lot.

"Mr. and Mrs. Burton were walking their dog this evening and found the body."

"Who is it?" I asked, a little afraid of what the answer would be.

"That's the interesting part. He still has his wallet on him. Name's Pablo Moreno. Has an Atlanta address, for what that's worth. Long rap sheet. Drugs, assault and a slew of petty crimes."

"What happened to him?"

"Also interesting. He appears to have been hit by a car and run over... repeatedly. Now that's just my amateur assessment, but I'm willing to bet on it."

"Nobody else has reported it?"

"No one but the Burtons."

I was trying to make sense of this. "Seems a little much to believe it was an accident."

"Take one look at the body and you'll know that this was no boating accident. Maybe they didn't mean to hit him the first time, but the follow-up was clearly deliberate."

I called Darlene and filled her in. She was in the middle of dinner, so I told her to take her time. We wouldn't be able to get to the body for a while, as the crime scene unit was still on its way.

We walked back over to the Burtons and I got their story. It was pretty basic—hadn't heard anything or seen anything until their dog, a black Lab named Mountain, had sniffed his way to the body. I got their contact info and let them go.

I sat in Pete's car while we waited for Shantel and Marcus to set up the lights and photograph the scene. I texted Cara to assure her that, as far as I knew, no one from the clinic had been hurt, then I took a look at Moreno's priors. Pete hadn't exaggerated. This was one bad dude. Only twenty-seven years-old and, at the rate he was going, it would have been clear to anyone that it was only a matter of time until found himself with a tag on his toe. But why here and why now?

"What's happened now?" I heard someone ask. I looked up and saw Dr. Barnhill standing by the car's window, staring at his clinic. He was obviously shaken up, and who could blame him?

I got out and filled him in on what we knew so far, which wasn't much.

"So, I'm confused. Do you think this has anything to do with the other death?"

"I'm about ninety percent sure that's the case. The odds that you would end up with two dead bodies on your property in less than a week, and have them *not* be related, are highly unlikely." I was really beginning to wonder what type of illegal activity was taking place here. Something seemed to be drawing bad guys like flies to garbage. "We'll know more when we've had a chance to look at the body."

"You keep saying that you're going to know more, but that never seems to happen," Dr. Barnhill said with a sigh. He was upset and had every right to be.

Shantel and Marcus were busy taking pictures when Darlene drove up. By the time I finished bringing her up to speed with the little bit that we knew, Shantel gave us the thumbs-up to view the body.

Wearing protective booties and walking on a narrow path, we approached the figure. Moreno had long black hair and, in the glare of the work lights, I could see numerous tattoos covering his face and neck. Most of them looked homemade, or even like prison tats. He was wearing a denim cowboy-style shirt and jeans, both thoroughly soaked in blood. His chest and stomach were crushed.

"I'd say that he was knocked to the ground and then run over. But that's just my guess," I snarked.

"Or an elephant stomped on him," Darlene suggested. "Seriously, whoever did this must have run over him three or four times."

"Puts the over in overkill. How often do guys like this work alone?" I asked.

"What are you thinking?" Pete asked.

"Honestly, I don't know," I said. Looking at the body and considering his priors, I knew that I needed to call Eddie sooner rather than later. "This guy and his record suggest that drugs are part of this."

"A car-jacking gone bad?" Darlene said. She was always willing to throw out ideas and she kept an open mind—two things that made her a good partner.

"Or something related to the earlier killing," I said.

"I'm glad this is your case and not mine," Pete said emphatically.

I walked back to Dr. Barnhill and told him a little of what we'd found. "Would you mind calling your employees and making sure that everyone is safe? I was with Cara so you don't need to call her, but make sure that all of the others are okay."

"Of course. I should have thought of that."

"We'll also need you to let us into the building in a little while so we can check the security camera footage."

"I don't know how much of the parking lot it covers," he said worriedly as he fumbled with his phone. I left him to make his calls.

A few minutes later he was back at my side. "Sandra didn't answer, but I left a message for her. I got ahold of everyone else."

"Okay, let's go inside and have a look at the camera footage."

We went around to the back door, which Marcus had already dusted for prints. There weren't any signs of a break-in, but there hadn't been any last time either. The dogs were barking up a storm as we opened the door and turned on the lights. I followed Marcus, who was videotaping everything as we went.

"Let me know if anything looks out of place," I told Dr. Barnhill.

"Everything looks normal." His voice was slightly shaky and I worried about him. I wondered how good his health was. This kind of stress could take someone down fast.

He unlocked his office. Inside was a new cabinet equipped with fans to vent the heat from the computer equipment. "Everything is locked in here now," he said, opening the cabinet.

I looked at the monitor and realized I didn't want to touch any of it for fear of screwing something up. The last thing in the world I needed to do was erase evidence.

"I'll call Lionel, our IT expert."

When I got Lionel on the phone, it sounded like he was at a party or a bar.

"Party," he confirmed. "But I've only been nursing a beer."

"That's what they all say. Can you get over here as soon as possible?"

"Lucky for you I'm in Calhoun. Give me half an hour."

Good as his word, he showed up in twenty minutes. By that time, Darlene and Pete had joined us in front of the computer.

"Is that you?" I asked Lionel, smelling a perfume that, to my country nose, didn't seem very manly.

"I told you, I was at a party," he said with a grin. He was short, dark and kept his hair cropped close to his skull. He always dressed well, but tonight he'd gone above and beyond in a silk shirt and dress slacks, which were made a bit comical with the addition of booties and rubber gloves. "Now get out of my way and let me work my magic."

"It's not like you have to hack the system," Darlene told him.

"Anytime I touch a keyboard, it's magic," he said, raising his eyebrows suggestively.

"Just show us the video," I said.

Lionel pulled up the video from several different cameras. We could see Sandra working around the office for about an hour after everyone else had left.

"Did you know that she was going to be working late?" I asked Dr. Barnhill.

"Yes. She was catching up on some record-keeping that fell through the cracks when we had to move to the Tallahassee clinic."

While Sandra finished her work in one frame, we could see the occasional figure pass under the camera outside. Two different men appeared to be hanging around outside of the clinic. The first time we saw them, they were wearing hoodies and came creeping up to the building to peek into the windows. It wasn't quite dark yet, but with the hoodies it was impossible to make out their faces. Soon it became clear that they were aware of the cameras and, about five minutes before Sandra left the office, the camera focused on the parking lot went black. Lionel confirmed via the timestamp that the camera was still recording, but the lens saw nothing.

"Paint," he said. It wouldn't have been a hard job to reach up and spray the camera that was only seven or eight feet off of the ground on the single-story building.

The last image we had was of Sandra leaving through the front door, then nothing else after that. Before the parking lot camera had gone black, we'd been able to see Sandra's car in the lot. I had no doubt it was hers, as she was the only person in the county I knew of who drove a smart car. But now there was no trace of the car or Sandra.

"We need to put out a BOLO on her car," I said.

"Apparently she managed to fight them off long enough to get to her car and knock one of them down and kill him," Darlene observed.

"I don't know. These are pretty bad hombres. Maybe Moreno's partner was at the wheel and drove over him," Pete said.

"Possibly... If he was hurt and his partner didn't want to leave a wounded man behind who might talk," I said, following Pete's train of thought.

"Either way, it looks like Sandra's been abducted." Darlene got on her radio and started giving information to dispatch.

"We need to tell Shantel to look for any blood outside and sample it. Obviously Moreno left a bunch, but we need to find out if Sandra was injured during the attack," Pete said.

"The question is why? Why abduct her? Was that the original plan on Tuesday and Rybeck messed it up?"

"Maybe he had the same partner as Moreno and the guy just doesn't play well with others," Pete answered.

I called Dad and filled him in on the situation. With Sandra apparently abducted, we could call in the FBI. Dad said he'd arrange a conference call with them first thing in the morning to determine whether they should come in on the investigation or just advise and assist.

Having heard my end of the conversation, Darlene said, "Here we go again. Wondering if we should give up control of an investigation to another agency."

"And deep down we're all control freaks," I said with a

sigh, hating to admit it.

"'Merica. Everyone wants to be the guy who carries the ball across the goal line."

"You're telling me that we need to be team players. You don't have to convince me. Sandra's life is on the line. I won't let my ego get in the way."

"I didn't know you had an ego," she kidded me.

"He does have one," Pete, who'd been standing nearby and listening in, tossed out.

"Keep it up, guys and gals. Someday you won't have ol' Larry to kick around anymore. Damn it!"

"What?"

"I need to let Cara know about Sandra. She's going to take it hard and I don't want to wait until I come dragging in at four in the morning. It's late enough already." I pulled out my phone and went outside where I'd have a little privacy.

I filled Cara in as gently as I could. "At this point we don't know much more than that Sandra appears to have been caught up in whatever happened here tonight, and now no one can contact her."

"I can't believe this." Cara's voice cracked. I wished I could have been there to comfort her. Phones are a such poor way to communicate bad news.

"You know we'll do everything we can to get her back safely."

"I trust you."

"Have your parents settled in?" Even though I felt imposed upon, right now I was glad that they were there for Cara.

"Oh, yes. They've gone full native in the front yard. And Dad is even more worried about me now."

"I'm not feeling that good myself about you working here. I wish your training with Pete was a little further along," I said, thinking about her range time with Pete, who was also the department's firearms instructor.

"We can't close up. We're the only vet in town. And while some of our clients and patients can get to Tallahassee, the trip is too much of a burden on the older and poorer ones."

"We aren't going to press Dr. Barnhill on it yet. He can do what he thinks is best. I *am* going to make sure that the security measures are the best that they can be. I'm kicking myself for not surveying the whole system after Tuesday."

"You can't be too mad at yourself. You're the one that's always talking about how any security system can be breached. The better ones just take more time," Cara said, repeating one of my favorite talking points.

"Wow, you do listen to me."

"Yeah, sometimes. Selective hearing and all that," she said, sounding a little more like her old self.

"I have to go. The coroner's people are here."

After hanging up with Cara, I went over and checked in with the two assistants that Dr. Darzi had sent. I wasn't surprised that the coroner didn't drag himself over here at this hour.

CHAPTER ELEVEN

Half an hour after they had arrived, one of Darzi's assistants walked over to me, holding out Moreno's phone in a plastic bag.

"It was in his pocket. I don't know how it didn't get crushed," he said, handing me the evidence bag. "That is the most runned-over person I've ever seen."

I thanked him for the phone. It was a burner, but there were several recent calls on it. One was from a Columbus number. *Are we getting somewhere?* I wondered. Of course, all of the numbers he'd called could have been to burner phones as well, which would mean that we still didn't have much. But a man could dream.

Darlene and I had told Pete that he could leave everything in our capable hands, but as he was on call anyway, he said he'd hang out for a while and help with crowd control. This last was a joke. We'd had a few gawkers, but they were all in cars. At one point, Deputy Sanderson had to tell drivers to move on, but that was the sum total of the traffic congestion.

Darlene, Pete, Shantel, Marcus and I combed the area around the building with flashlights, looking under all the bushes for anything that might have been left before or during the struggle... or, at least, what we were assuming had been a struggle. It was difficult work in the dark, even with our high-powered flashlights.

"Got something!" Pete called out from the bushes near the front of the building.

We all came over and Marcus photographed the items that Pete had found. They were scattered over a square yard under the hawthorn. There was a small clutch purse, a wallet and a compact. We agreed that the wallet and the compact had probably come out of the purse when it was dropped in the bushes. We figured that Sandra had been grabbed as she came out the front door. The items were only a few feet from the steps leading to the small porch.

We carefully picked up each item after everything was photographed and measured. I wasn't surprised that we didn't find her phone in her purse. Even under the bushes, I'd have heard it ring when Dr. Barnhill had tried to call her. The wallet seemed to be complete with Sandra's driver's license and an array of credit cards. And, of course, we didn't find any keys. Sandra would have still had the keys in her hand after locking the front door, and either she or one of the bad guys had used them to run over Moreno and drive off in her car.

"They were targeting Sandra," I stated with more certainty than I felt. Nothing about this case seemed to follow the rules.

"Seems logical from what we saw on the video," Darlene concurred.

"That's the first assumption. The second is that the two deaths are related."

"A safe premise, I'd say." Darlene had gone into full Dr. Watson mode.

"Therefore we should find somewhere in their pasts that Rybeck's, Moreno's and Sandra's trails intersect."

"Whoa, cowboy," Darlene said, dropping the Watson act. "I agree in principle, but it also looks like Moreno and his fellow traveler may have just been hired guns. Sandra might not have ever seen them before or know who they are. The link could be the guy that hired them."

"A small wrench thrown into my carefully built plan."

Pete chimed in. "Look at the three of them. The two victims are guys with criminal pasts. Different in the degree of priors, but still solid histories. The third, Sandra, doesn't *appear* to have a criminal background. I'd say that's where you need to look."

The three of us had been leaning against my car, watching Darzi's guys pick up the body bag containing what was left of Moreno and set it on a stretcher. They'd had a few awkward moments, since his bones from the shoulder down to the pelvis had been pulverized. The middle part of the body had lacked the crucial support of a skeleton when they'd tried to lift it.

"I see your point. Somewhere, Sandra has to have come into contact with something illicit and we just need to discover what that was," I said, warming to the idea.

"That is, if Moreno and his friend were specifically targeting Sandra and not just any employee of the clinic," Darlene pointed out.

"You have a point," Pete admitted.

"She always has to throw a fly into the ointment," I kidded.

"And there is the one in ten thousand chance that Moreno and company are just a couple of badasses on the make and that this is all a coincidence."

"Nope," I said.

"Nyet," Pete chimed in.

"Yeah, me neither," Darlene said with a grin. "Just trying to stir up more flies."

I sobered up. "We're joking, but Sandra's life could be in danger. Were you able to get the warrant for her phone records?" I asked Darlene.

"I did, and I was able to reach someone high enough up at the phone company that they could give orders. In theory, we should be getting a report soon of the last calls made from and to her phone. Also, they're going to try to get us the ping data starting at the time of the abduction."

"Gives us some chance of tracking her," Pete said.

"I also got dispatch to call and confirm the BOLO on the car out to two hundred miles. They complained that that meant about fifty law enforcement agencies they'd have to call, but I don't want it left to a computer alert." Like anyone whose job demands more attention than any one human can possibly give it, LEOs tend to respond quickest to what is stuck under their noses and marked urgent.

"I don't want to sit here doing nothing. I'm going to check some of the security footage from businesses in the neighborhood," I said. "Maybe we can at least get an idea of the direction they headed leaving town."

"I'll go south if you go north. Though some of them will be long closed, like the bank," Darlene said.

"This is an emergency. We'll use the emergency contact numbers and get someone out here. They certainly don't mind getting us out of bed to check on their banks or stores a dozen times in a month because they're too busy or too cheap to get their alarms fixed, so I don't care if I spoil their Friday evening plans," I said boldly. I knew that, even though Dad was relying on local businessmen to back him in the fall election, he'd never let that stop him from kicking butt to save someone who'd been abducted.

"I'll stay here and help Shantel and Marcus finish up," Pete said, hoisting himself off of the car. They were just starting to collect samples from the numerous pools of blood. I hoped that none of the blood was Sandra's. If it was, then we might have already been too late.

I drove away from the clinic and made note of a couple of businesses that were already closed but might have cameras pointed toward the street. The first place I came to that was open, and that I knew had cameras facing the parking lot that would pick up north-bound traffic, was the Fast Mart.

I pulled into a parking space and the four guys and a girl

loitering in front of the building slinked around the edge and disappeared into the darkness.

"Welcome to Fast Mart," said the young clerk when I walked in. "Free coffee if you want it."

The management was always very friendly to law enforcement, but never followed through on the things we advised them to do to improve their clientele. I suspected that they didn't mind taking money from druggies, but that they just wished they'd stop hanging around making the place look bad.

"I need to see your security footage from earlier tonight," I told the clerk. He looked like he spent a bit too much time in the candy aisle, but at least they didn't have someone with "target" written all over them working behind the counter on a Friday night.

"Sure. I just got to call the manager. He's got the keys to the back room," he said, keeping one eye on the corner ceiling mirror where we could see a young mother carrying a baby. Every twenty seconds she'd glace toward him. He leaned forward and said confidentially, "You wouldn't believe it, but sometimes the ones with babies are the worst shoplifters."

"Tell the manager that this is an emergency and someone's life is in danger."

"Yeah, yeah, no problem." He pressed a button on his phone, talked for a minute and hung up. "He's on his way. It's not a problem since he does a couple of deposits on Friday and Saturday anyway."

They need a drop safe, I thought, but didn't get into it. At least they weren't letting the money pile up inside the store

The manager arrived ten minutes later and didn't even grumble when he let me into the back room.

"You're lucky. I know how to review the night's footage. Anything more complicated and I'd need to call in my nephew."

Does everyone rely on their younger family members to run their security systems? I wondered.

It was easy to zero in on the correct time in the video, as we knew exactly when Sandra had been attacked. Sure enough, a car matching Sandra's 2014 silver smart car passed the camera going north just a few minutes later. Unfortunately, the Fast Mart was on the north-bound side of the road and the angle of the camera couldn't pick up the driver's face.

I ran the footage back and forth a dozen times. It looked like something, or someone, was in the passenger seat, but it could have been anything: a box, groceries, a person lying down in the seat. The car was so damn small that it was impossible to tell.

I thanked the manager and asked for a copy of the video. As soon as I was back in my car, I called dispatch and asked them nicely to contact the jurisdictions north of Adams County and alert them that Sandra's car was last seen headed in their direction. I promised pastries for everyone in dispatch.

I also let Darlene know that I'd gotten a look at the car headed north, so that she could abandon her fruitless south-bound search. She told me that she'd meet me at the bank two blocks from the Fast Mart.

An hour later, Darlene and I were viewing very rough footage of the driver that a very unhappy bank manager had pulled from a camera in their lot.

"What do you think?" I asked Darlene.

"I'd say the driver is female. But, honestly, that's only an impression."

"What about a passenger?"

"There might be one, or it could just be an artifact of the light and pixilation." With the tinted windows rolled up, there was a lot of reflection from the streetlights.

"Which leaves us where?" I asked, knowing that we still had no answers to any of the important questions.

"Best case, Sandra is driving by herself, which doesn't make a lot of sense. Next possibility, she's driving and her abductor is in the seat next to her with a gun. I put that pretty high on the probability scale. Or, the other assailant appears to be female and Sandra is tied up in the trunk."

"Can you even get someone in the trunk of a smart car?" I asked

"Good question. Maybe not," Darlene said as we both pondered the dimensions of the little car.

We were trying to decide where to go next when we both got a text from Pete calling us back to the clinic ASAP. When we arrived, we saw that floodlights had been set up on the next block behind the clinic. Pete was putting up crime scene tape as Marcus studied something on the pavement.

"Nothin' can be easy with you," Shantel said as she walked up to my car. "Wait until you see what Pete found for you. You need to start hanging around with an investigator that has some good luck." This last was directed to Darlene. "This man hasn't ever caught a murder that didn't turn into a five alarm fire."

Pete stopped putting up the tape when he saw us. "Blood. It took us a while to find the trail because Sandra's car must have driven through it. I followed it back here." He pointed to a spot in the street a car's width from the curb. "Someone who was bleeding got into a car parked right there."

My mind ran through a multitude of scenarios that would explain the puddle of blood, but none of them made a lot of sense. I looked over at Darlene, who appeared as confused as I felt. "A fourth person?" I asked her.

"If we hadn't found that footage, I might think that Sandra drove off and this person," she pointed at the blood, "ran over here, got in a car and chased her. But the driver of the smart car didn't seem to be in any rush."

"No. And there didn't appear to be a car behind it in pursuit. When I looked at the Fast Mart video, I let several seconds pass before rewinding."

"But if Sandra drove off by herself, then why didn't she call someone or go to the police station or our office?"

"Maybe there was a third abductor."

"That makes the most sense. All three came from this car—including the ill-fated Pablo Moreno—walked over to the clinic, ambushed Sandra, things went wrong and Moreno was killed while one of the other men was hurt. The third man drove off in Sandra's car while the other man, left alive, retrieved the car they came in." Darlene spelled it out thoughtfully.

"Makes as much sense as anything else."

"It's a bit crazy. But we've seen bad guys come up with some elaborate and stupid plans in the past."

"All of this does give us a little more hope. If we can find someone who saw this car, then we'll have another clue we can chase," I said.

"And we have one of the other perp's DNA," Darlene said, pointing to the blood.

"Thanks, guys. You all were making me feel like I was just complicating your life. But see, I'm really just trying to help," Pete said.

An hour later we received a report from the cell phone company, including the fact that the last ping from Sandra's phone was within a mile radius of Calhoun, about ten minutes after she walked out of the vet clinic. Other than Dr. Barnhill's attempt to contact her, there were no calls between the time everyone else had left the clinic and the time of the last ping. Honestly, there was very little activity at all for a person of her age. The report indicated that she was in the bottom ten percent of phone usage for her demographic. *What does that mean?* I wondered.

With nothing else that we could accomplish before daylight, I finally headed home a little after three. I tried to ignore the giant teepee—err, yurt—in the front yard. I opened the door as quietly as possible and soft-stepped my way into the bedroom, but I heard Cara turn over.

"Larry?"

"I didn't want to wake you."

"I haven't really been sleeping. How are you?"

96

"Just tired. We still haven't found Sandra," I told her.

"Dr. Barnhill called and said that we'd route most of our patients into Tallahassee again. Tomorrow's appointments are mostly routine for people who can't make it in during the week, so they can be rescheduled. We really just can't be open like nothing has happened."

She was sitting up in bed now as I undressed and got in beside her. The light from the moon streamed through the window, casting everything in a soft blue light.

She reached for my hand. "And I feel awful worrying about schedules and clinic details when poor Sandra…"

"There isn't anything else we can do until morning," I told her gently. "I need to grab a little sleep. And so do you."

We kissed and embraced for a moment before rolling into our own spaces on the bed, trying to sleep as soundly as we could when people we knew were in danger and problems were left unsolved.

CHAPTER TWELVE

On Saturday I was up before eight. As I started to sit down at the table with a bowl of cereal and some toast, I heard a soft knocking at the door. *Henry or Anna?* I wondered. When I opened the door I learned that I was lucky twice. Both of them were standing on my small porch.

"I saw your light come on. I thought you'd like something good for breakfast," Anna said, gently easing her way past me into the house. She was carrying a small cast iron Dutch oven in her gloved hands. "Fresh oatmeal. A friend of our sends it to us by the twenty-five-pound bag. I put in some fresh fruit."

"And I want to talk to you about Cara's safety," Henry said in a serious tone as he also tried to ease past me. However, the space between me and the door wasn't big enough for him to squeeze his bulk through. I relented and moved back, giving him enough room to come in.

"I don't have much time. I really need to get to work," I said to both of them.

Anna ignored me and tossed out my cereal.

"Hey, save some of the milk for Ivy," I said, really wanting to protest that *I'd* wanted the cereal.

Ivy was watching the two intruders from her perch on

the back of the couch, her eyes guarded and her ears slightly swept back. *At least one occupant of the house feels the way I do*, I thought.

Alvin, on the other hand, was fawning all over them, no doubt because Henry kept a supply of homemade venison jerky in a bag in his pocket. He reached in and took out a small piece, handing it to the dog, who instantly looked like he had been transported to a higher celestial plane.

"Milk isn't good for her. Besides, your cereal is full of refined sugar and all kinds of bad things," Anna chided me.

"But…"

"I brought her a little treat." Anna withdrew a small heart-shaped fabric pouch from her pocket. "My own special catnip." She went over and laid the heart on the arm of the couch.

Ivy moved back warily, but a moment later I saw her tilt her head up and sniff the air. Suddenly she hopped down from the back of the couch and hooked the heart with a claw, pulling it down into the couch beside her. Before my eyes, she joined Alvin in pure bliss. I looked at her and she looked back at me, her eyes glassy and dilated as she sniffed and rubbed against the heart. I was alone.

"Sit," Anna ordered. "Five minutes and I'll have this heated up."

A bleary-eyed Cara came stumbling out of the bedroom. I fought the urge to glare at her. This wasn't her fault… at least not completely.

"I really don't have much time," I said as sternly as I could without sounding like a total asshole.

"We need to talk about Cara's safety," Henry repeated, leaning across the table. "There's a killer stalking that vet and I'm not going to let her go back there unprotected." He was in full papa bear mode. Cara stayed out of it, trying to get around her mother to the coffee.

"I understand. They aren't going to be open for business today, and I agree that no one should be alone at the clinic until we figure out exactly what's going on."

"What progress have you made in the investigation?" he asked me.

None at all with me sitting here talking to you, I wanted to say. What I actually said was, "We have some leads, but nothing that suggests an arrest is going to happen anytime soon."

"Bad news," he grumbled as Anna set down a bowl of oatmeal in front of me.

"And here's some honey from another friend of ours. The bees gather nectar from the wild flowers on Paynes Prairie."

She handed me a small jar out of the same voluminous pocket that she'd produced the heart for Ivy. I poured a little of the honey on the oatmeal and stirred it up before tasting it.

"It's good, thank you," I said honestly.

Behind her mother's back, Cara was making frantic signs at me and mouthing: *No*. Anna whirled around.

"I saw that," she said, threatening to give Cara a smack with the spoon she had in her hand.

"I was just trying to warn him that if he complimented you we'd have you over here feeding us all the time," Cara said lightly.

"Good food is the foundation of life."

Cara joined me at the table and a bowl of oatmeal was quickly set in front of her too.

"And you're going to eat that," Anna said as only a mother can.

I had finished mine. "I really have to go," I said, getting up.

"I'll keep an eye on Cara," Henry said as he ate.

Cara rolled her eyes a bit, but she couldn't hide a small smile. Who wouldn't be nervous after all the deaths at the clinic? Henry would make a formidable body guard.

"That'll be great," I said, winking as I caught Cara's eye. I gave her a kiss and headed for the door.

Darlene was already at her desk when I got to the office.

When does she sleep? I wondered. I suppose it wasn't easy to turn off all that nervous energy.

"We have a conference call with the FBI in your father's office in half an hour." As she said it, my phone's text alert went off, letting me know that I had a message saying exactly the same thing. Sometimes I couldn't decide if modern technology was really more efficient or not.

"What are we going to push for?" I asked Darlene.

"I say shoot for the moon. The full FBI package. Officers on site and full resources."

"That would be great, but they can be a bit picky about the details sometimes."

"It's true that we don't have absolute proof that she was kidnapped, but we do have a boatload of circumstantial evidence."

"I just wish we had a third man on our surveillance footage," I said.

We got to Dad's office five minutes early and spent most of that time going through the rigorous Great Dane greeting ritual with Mauser. The ritual mostly involved everyone telling him that he was a good boy while he trotted from person to person, drooling and leaning on them.

From the outside, having the big monster around might've appeared unprofessional and a hindrance to a well-run office. However, Mauser was Dad's secret weapon. Citizens would come into his office ready to complain about something, and the next thing they knew, they were engaged in a conversation about Mauser's eating habits or where Dad found collars large enough to fit him. After that, Dad would ask them what was wrong and a fairly civil discussion would take place, the person having been derailed by Mauser's presence long enough for their anger to defuse.

Of course, there were occasions when Dad had to talk with people in another office because they were too frightened to meet Mauser. One of the standard briefings for anyone requesting a meeting with the sheriff was a warning that a giant canine lurked on the other side of the door.

The call connected right on time. After introductions and preliminaries, we got down to business. "From what you've said, I'm not sure that I can justify our involvement," Special Agent in Charge Alverado informed us.

"To our knowledge, this young woman has not been involved in any criminal activities," Dad said, looking at us as we nodded in agreement. "So it seems highly unlikely that she would just drive off after being assaulted by two men."

I cringed as he referenced two men, since our working theory was that there had been three. The agent picked right up on that too.

"You say two men. In the brief you emailed me, I see you've noted one is dead and you have the second leaving in the car that the assailants presumably arrived in. If that's the case, then there wasn't anyone left to kidnap the woman."

"When I said two, I meant the two we have on surveillance cameras. We believe that there must have been third person involved."

"You have no evidence of a third attacker. You only believe that there was one because you want to assume that the woman was abducted. It's a circular argument."

"She left her purse and wallet behind."

"Again, not proof of an abduction."

The agent was being a real hardass. Usually they're a little more open to marginal cases. I wondered what kind of budget smackdown he'd recently received. Or maybe he resented working on a Saturday. Then I decided I was being unfair to a guy who was probably just doing his job.

"Moreno was a serious offender. No doubt moving drugs on a regional level," Dad pressed.

"From his record he was certainly not a nice guy. It would be fair to call him extremely dangerous, but he's dead. I'd be glad to shake the lady's hand if she put him on the slab. I think there is at least a fifty-fifty chance that she decided on her own not to hang around. Now, if you want to pursue the drug angle then you need to call the DEA. I hate to be this cut-and-dried, but we don't have the resources to investigate cases that don't have a hook for us. Show me something that moves the needle in the direction of a kidnapping and I'll be more than glad to shift assistance your way." Alverado was beginning to sound irritated that we were still talking to him.

"I understand," Dad said, running up the white flag.

A few goodbyes later and the call was disconnected.

"The FBI is out for the moment," Dad said curtly. The phone call had left him grinding his teeth. He hated to be dismissed out of hand.

"Then our first mission is to dig into Sandra's background. We need to know if she was the target of the attack from the beginning or if she just presented herself as a possible victim by being alone in the office," I said.

"And we can't ignore the possibility that there is someone with a vendetta against the clinic or the Barnhills. So questioning them again with an eye toward enemies that they might have is high on the list too," Darlene put in.

"I can't get around the fact that she killed Moreno and wounded another assailant," Dad said.

"An in-depth look into her background might help to explain that."

"What? Like she worked for the CIA?" Dad asked skeptically.

"Stranger things have happened. Maybe she's ex-law enforcement and is part of a witness protection program. Actually, that would explain why she didn't hang around and talk with us," I said, liking the idea after having said it out loud. However, from his face I could tell that Dad was doubtful. "I'll pick Cara's brain too. They've spent a bit of time together."

"I met Sandra a couple of times when I took Mauser to the vet. I never did more than say hi to her, but I'm not sure I can see her as an LEO. But maybe."

"I still think there is a good chance she was abducted," I said. "And we may be presuming too much. Maybe the bad guys got in a fight among themselves. It wouldn't be the first time. I remember a burglary where they found both of the guys dead in the house. They'd gotten into an argument over a stereo and stabbed each other to death."

"I want to go over the video from the clinic and see if we can pick up any other clues as to what happened," Darlene said. "We're also going to look for any more cameras that might have caught sight of them or their cars. And we'll canvass the neighborhood this morning to see if anyone has a description of the car that the bad guys used."

"Shantel's offered to put a rush on the bloodwork so we can find out, first, if Sandra was injured and, second, if we can prove that another person was involved. If that blood trail came from the other attacker, then we'll be able to get a DNA profile. I think it's safe to assume that the other guy in the hoodie has a record. So that's one route we can go to put a name on him."

"If you come up with a fourth person's blood, I'd be willing to go back to the FBI," Dad said. I knew he'd enjoy having another go at Mister Special Agent in Charge, especially with a few more arrows in his quiver.

"One of us should probably go up to Columbus and ask some questions," I said, getting the *How much will that cost?* look from Dad.

"Day trip. We can't afford the hotel and we can't afford to be an investigator short right now," he said in his gruffest bookkeeper tone. "What about the DEA?"

"The trip to Columbus might help to answer that. If our first victim was working for drug dealers and our second victim was clearly involved in drugs, then this is most likely a drug case and calling in the DEA makes sense," I said.

"I'll call them and see if they're interested in the fact that Moreno is dead. It's possible that he was the subject of an ongoing investigation," Darlene offered.

"Keep me posted," Dad said, which was our cue to leave. We were followed out the door by the sound of Mauser snoring away on his twin mattress.

We hit the phones when we got back to our desks. My

first call was to Eddie, my CI, and I wasn't surprised when I had to leave a message for him. But he shocked me by calling back almost immediately.

"Got your message."

"I'm going to send you some names and pictures."

"You know I'm trying to go clean, right?" he asked, doing his sad Eddie routine. He really should have been an actor.

"I know, Eddie. I appreciate your willingness to mix with addicts to get information for me."

"How much do you appreciate it?" he said, sounding less sad and more greedy.

"Some. But I would think you'd have more money now that you aren't snorting it or injecting it into your body."

"Come on, man! You know that my family's spending a ton on lawyers. I can't get a dime from any of them now."

"If they knew how much you helped to put them in the tight spot they're in, you wouldn't need money ever again," I told him.

"Don't even joke about that."

"Mum's the word. Look, this is important, or I wouldn't ask. And I'll make sure you get a reasonable reward for the help that you provide. I've always been fair, haven't I?"

"Whatever," he said grudgingly. "Send the pictures. I'll see what I can do."

I texted him pictures of Sandra, Rybeck and Moreno, then set to work making calls to trace Sandra's work history. Since Code Red Medical Supply, the company she'd worked for in Macon, had since gone bankrupt, I had to spend some time tracking down one of the former owners.

"Sandra. Yes, she worked for us. A very good office manager. It's all so sad," Dennis Moss said. I could almost hear him shaking his head over the phone. I figured he was referring to the loss of the company.

"She left when the company closed down?" I asked and there was a long pause on the other end of the phone.

"What is this all about? Is her family trying to open a new

investigation into the accident?" Moss asked, leaving me confused.

"What accident?"

"How do I know you're even a deputy? And why in the world would a sheriff's office in Florida be interested in Sandra now?" Moss was sounding more and more suspicious.

"Check online, find the number for the Adams County Sheriff's Office, call it and ask to speak with Larry Macklin," I told him, actually appreciating someone who was savvy enough to question a phone call out of the blue. It's the gullible witnesses that can give the worst information.

"I hate to be this way, but I'm going to."

We hung up and a few minutes later my desk phone rang.

"So why are you interested in Sandra's death?" he asked when we'd completely established my identity. His question wasn't a surprise at this point. During the time that it took him to call me back, I'd been parsing what he said and was beginning to have my doubts about Sandra.

"Could you tell me exactly what happened to Sandra?" I asked.

"I guess it was about a month after we had closed down. Sandra was in her car on I-75, just north of Macon. I think she was going to Atlanta for a job interview. The morning was foggy, the road damp. The highway patrol said she ran off the road and hit some trees pretty much head-on. She died instantly. There were some malicious rumors that she killed herself, but I doubt it. Sandra was always very upbeat, and it wasn't like she'd been out of work for that long."

I asked him for a description of Sandra, and she was a fair match for ours with a few minor differences. I thanked Moss for his time, apologizing that I couldn't give him any more information about an active investigation.

I hung up and settled back in my seat, thinking about the interviews with Sandra and Dr. Barnhill. How had she gotten her references? She'd probably given Dr. Barnhill a false letter of reference with the number of someone who would vouch for her in the letterhead. A clever person would have been able to come up with a dozen different ways.

I was just getting up to share what I'd learned with Darlene when my phone rang with a call from Shantel.

"You need to come back here," she said.

When you get a command from Shantel, you don't question it. "On my way."

CHAPTER THIRTEEN

I picked up Darlene when I walked by her desk and told her that we now had a mystery woman.

"That opens things up," she said.

When we got back to the evidence room, Shantel was standing at the counter with a microscope. "I was just double-checking, but as soon as I looked at it in daylight, I knew," she said, waving at the counter.

I looked at the microscope and saw a driver's license on the plate. "Let me guess. Sandra's driver's license isn't the real deal."

"Got it in one," Shantel congratulated me, and I explained what I'd just learned about Sandra's résumé.

"Which explains why she was willing to leave it in the bushes. I wonder if she had another ID waiting for her?" Darlene said.

"Great, now we don't even know who we're looking for," I grumbled.

"Kicks the kidnapping theory down a notch or two," Darlene admitted.

"FBI coming in?" Shantel asked. Darlene and I both shook our heads.

"Looks like she high-tailed it," Darlene said.

"If drug dealers are after her, then maybe she stole money or drugs," I suggested.

"Or both."

"I guess there's a chance she's in the witness protection program."

"If that's the case, then shouldn't the U.S. Marshals be getting in touch with you? And wouldn't she have contacted them after the first death?" Shantel asked.

"Unless she was doing something she shouldn't have under the rules of the program. And, remember, if we're right then she killed the first guy, but only after she let him in," I said.

"Besides, the U.S. Marshals don't make fake drivers' licenses," Darlene said. "With them you get the real deal."

"Just when I think we're close to getting some answers, a million more questions pop up," I sighed.

"We have two victims. We know who they are. I say we run them down as best we can. I already left a message with the DEA letting them know that we've confirmed the death of Pablo Moreno. We'll see if they have any interest in him."

"The way this investigation is going, I expect that once we check his prints we'll find out that Moreno isn't really Moreno." His prints wouldn't be checked until Dr. Darzi had conducted his full examination and had a chance to extract any evidence that might have been on the victim's hands or under his fingernails.

"I think we matched up the tattoos pretty well. I'm not worried about that," Darlene said.

"Oh, I got a text from Darzi this morning. He's put the autopsy off until Monday. Victims of a multi-car accident on I-10 are taking precedence."

We thanked Shantel and headed back to our desks.

"Do you want to flip a coin for who goes to Columbus?" Darlene asked me. Before I could answer, dispatch called to report that they'd tracked down one of Moreno's relatives and gave me the number of a cousin who was expecting our call.

I held the phone out to Darlene, but she shook her head. She hated to do notifications. I didn't enjoy it either, but was willing to take one for the team.

"Is this Miguel Moreno?" I asked when my call was answered.

"Yes, what has happened?" The heavily accented voice on the other end of the line sounded anxious.

"I'm sorry to inform you that your cousin Pablo Moreno has been killed." I didn't try to sugar-coat something that wouldn't be made any better by euphemisms.

There was silence at the other end of the line, then finally, "I see." The voice was now resigned and sounded tired.

"You don't sound surprised."

"There were three brothers and a sister. Pablo was the last. They are all dead now. All were less than forty. No, I'm not surprised to hear that Pablo is gone. I was more surprised that he lived as long as he did."

"What did his other siblings die of?"

"Different things, but all the same. His brothers, they were working for bad people. One was killed in a car crash. The older brother was stabbed in prison. His sister. So sweet. Esther had black hair that reached to her waist. She died of a drug overdose, they said. But her soul had left her body long before that. The whole family was cursed." I could hear a little anger in his voice now.

"His mother and father?"

"Maria came to this country with the children when Angelo was killed in Mexico City. I don't know how he died. She came to live with my sister in Atlanta. Maria was a good, hard working mother, but she got sick, very, very sick, and died just five years later."

"When was the last time you saw Pablo?"

"At a party. Two years ago, maybe. He just got out of prison. My sister's son was graduating from college and she was having a celebration. Pablo showed up with some other cousins from his father's side of the family. He didn't stay long. I don't think there was enough partying for him, if you know what I mean."

"Where was he living?"

"I don't know. Somewhere here in Atlanta, I think. Maybe not. How much will it cost to bury him?" Miguel asked.

"I don't know. You'll have to contact a funeral home and they can make the arrangements."

"Me, I would say that you all could have him, but my sister, she's all about the family. She will never let him be buried in an unmarked grave. We will spend money better spent elsewhere to bring home a man who never thought of anyone but himself. It is crazy."

"Do you know of anyone who might have a better idea of what Pablo had been up to recently?"

"Maybe my sister might. I will have her give you a call."

"If you give me her number, I'll call her," I said.

"No, no. She will be very upset. She has a bigger heart than I do. I will tell her. She will call you today."

I gave him all of my contact information, wondering if I'd ever hear back from the sister.

Hanging up, I turned to Darlene. "It might be easier to do a notification when the person you're informing doesn't care, but it's still sad."

"I don't think you should lose much sleep over this creep," she reassured me.

I pulled up Moreno's arrest record and went over it again. The last couple of years were the longest time during his adult life that he hadn't had contact with law enforcement. I took this as an indication that he must have been working for someone who was paying him well and keeping him in line. But who?

"We never did decide on who was going to Columbus," I said, looking up from my monitor after a while.

"You go. I want to work on running down CCTV footage and canvassing the neighborhood around the clinic for anyone who might have seen our perp's car."

"Get Susan White or, better yet, Andy Martel to help you. Might improve his interpersonal skills." Martel was the most laconic deputy in the department.

"Thanks, but White will be fine. I've already called her. In fact, I'm meeting her in half an hour."

"Good hunting. I'll see about going up to Columbus to do some interviews tomorrow. Maybe we can get a better handle on our first victim." I wondered how Cara was going to like me skipping out on her for a whole day while her parents were here.

Thinking of her, I sent a text to check in with her. Though the clinic was technically closed, most of the staff had gone in to care for the boarders and patients, and to impose a little organization on chaos.

My father is stalking me!!!!! was the text that I got back.

I called her. "How's it going?"

"He's driving me crazy."

"I meant at the clinic," I said.

"Too depressing to talk about. I'd rather rant about my crazy father. We're going to try to be open on Monday, but Dr. Barnhill just looks so... confused... tired. I don't think he could take anything else happening."

"We're doing the best we can. Just a lot of dead ends. Look, I'm going to need to drive up to Columbus and talk to some people. Maybe as early as tomorrow."

"Take me with you," she pleaded.

"What about your parents?"

"Exactly, take me with you."

"You'd just leave them camping out in the front yard?" I was a bit surprised by her reaction. I knew that she'd moved up here from Gainesville because they were driving her a little crazy, but...

"They'll be fine." I could tell she wasn't kidding.

"I *am* going up there on business."

"We can take my car." It was a good argument. Dad certainly wouldn't mind if the department wasn't paying the whole bill for the trip.

"Maybe," I waffled and told her we'd talk about it more when I got home.

A few minutes after I hung up with Cara, Miguel Moreno's sister called me.

"My uncle, he was a nice man. His son had it rough growing up without a father and watching his mother die of cancer. I felt so sorry for him. Pablo did a lot of bad things, I know, but I remember the little boy who looked so scared hiding behind his mother. So much sadness in one family. Now they are all gone."

"Do you know where Pablo was living?"

"He called about six months ago. Said he just wanted me to know that he was doing okay. He gave me a phone number. Let me see." After some fumbling with her phone, she read out a number. "That's all I know. He never wrote letters or nothing."

I gave her the contact information for the morgue and a brief rundown of the process that she'd have to go through in order to get his body released to her. I told her that any funeral home would be glad to help her through the paperwork.

A quick search of area codes showed that the number Moreno had given his cousin was out of Columbus. Yet another arrow pointing that direction.

I grabbed a quick lunch, then decided to see if Darlene and White needed any help with their neighborhood canvassing. I found Darlene walking back to where her car was parked a couple of blocks from the vet clinic. She had just finished interviewing one neighbor who may or may not have seen or heard something at some time. Not exactly helpful.

"We're forgetting Wayne Dawson," I said.

"I was thinking about that. With everything pulling us toward Sandra, we've gotten sidetracked."

I took out my phone, found a number for Dawson and called him. He answered on the second ring.

"This is Wayne. What can I do for you?"

114

"Wayne, this is Deputy Larry Macklin. I'm an investigator with the sheriff's office. My partner and I would like to talk with you about the recent events at the clinic where your friend Gayle works."

"Oh, wow. Yeah, unbelievable. Man, if I can be of any help, sure. I'm in the middle of building a doghouse for Gayle's Yorkie, but sure, come on by. I'm in the garage." He gave me directions to his house, located about ten minutes outside of town.

Darlene radioed White to let her know that we were running off to question someone and would be back as soon as possible. I promised to help with the rest of the door-to-door work when we got done with Wayne.

The garage door was open when we pulled up outside his house. Wayne, wearing a polo shirt, flowered shorts and ear and eye protection, was cutting wood on an impressive table saw. The garage was a large, two-car affair filled with a lot of expensive DIY equipment. He didn't hear or see us until we were almost next to him. He jumped a little, stopped the saw and took off his eye and ear covers.

"Wayne Dawson," he said, sticking out his hand. Cara had been right—he had the good looks of a model. He wore a big, goofy smile on his face and had open, innocent eyes. We shook his hand and introduced ourselves.

"Wow. I've been telling Gayle she should take time off. Too scary. And last night, another body. Crazy. What can I do to help?"

I couldn't decide if the guy was really the goober he appeared to be or if he was just a great actor.

"If you could answer a few questions," Darlene said.

"Yeah, of course. Hey, would you like some tea? Come on in the house."

Of course, neither of us wanted the tea, but as investigators we didn't want to pass up the opportunity for a glimpse into a possible suspect's house. We followed him through a door out of the garage that led into a large utility room and then into an upscale kitchen. I was beginning to see why Cara thought Gayle was dating above her weight class.

"Nice house," I said.

"Oh, thanks. Yeah, I am sooo lucky. I got in on a start-up before I was even out of college. Me and my partner sold it for crazy money." He was pouring glasses of iced tea while he talked. "This is made with my own honey. I've got about forty hives out back and I've got fifty acres of wild flowers planted. I sell the honey. I could have started another company or worked for some Silicon Valley software giant, but all of that office stuff just depresses me. I love living in the country."

We accepted the glasses of tea. It was good, I had to give him that.

"So you just make honey now?" Darlene asked, sounding like she had more than a professional interest in what he did for a living.

"Yeah, like I said, I got lucky. I don't need to worry too much about money."

"How long have you been dating Gayle?" I wanted to get the conversation pointed in the right direction.

"A few months. She's super. We get along great," he said, and I had to wonder how and why.

We went over their trip and all of his details matched up with what Gayle had told us.

"Where were you yesterday evening?" I asked.

"Gayle and I went to dinner at Shula's 347 in Tallahassee and then to a movie. We saw *Singin' in the Rain*, part of a series where they screen old films. Wow, that was such a great movie. I just love to see those old musicals. We were singing the soundtrack all the way home. She stayed here last night," he finished with a stupid grin on his face.

The fourth ring of Hell would be being stuck in a car with Gayle and Wayne singing the hits from Singin' in the Rain, I thought. I was over them both. I didn't fully understand the relationship, but they deserved each other. I wasn't so sure that Darlene was over Wayne. I had to verbally poke her a couple of times to get her to leave.

In the car heading back to town, I heard her sigh. "Wow," she said, mimicking Wayne.

"Yeah, wow," I muttered. "Funny how a suspect can seem really promising until you talk to them."

"He may not be promising as a suspect, but wow," Darlene repeated.

"You're making me feel uncomfortable in my workplace," I told her.

"Sonny boy, I bet Wayne could make me feel wonderfully uncomfortable."

"Don't make me stop the car and throw up."

"I'll check out the alibi, just in case. Figures they'd go to Shula's 347. That must be one of the most expensive places in Tallahassee."

"I can't even afford to look at their menu."

Darlene shook her head to clear the Wayne fog. "Meanwhile, back on Earth," she said and pulled out a couple copies of a map of the neighborhood we'd be canvassing. Darlene circled a dozen houses for me to check, then I parked near the middle of the neighborhood and we went our separate ways.

CHAPTER FOURTEEN

Since it was Saturday, I stood as good a chance as any of finding folks at home. The day was pleasantly warm, with a soft breeze and just a few wispy clouds in the bright blue sky.

As I walked, I realized how much the world had changed in just a few decades, even in our small town. I could hear kids playing in backyards and a dog barking here and there, but there was nobody in the front yards of the houses I passed. From the street, the neighborhood looked almost deserted. I'd seen pictures and old home movies from when my dad and grandparents were kids, when all of the action had been in front of the house. Adults would sit and talk on the front porch while the children played in the yard. Salesmen came by with carts of fruits and vegetables or brushes and vacuums while mothers talked over the fences to their neighbors. But there was none of that anymore. Your friends lived across town or even in another city and your neighbors were just people that annoyed you or, at best, that you waved to on occasion.

There was no answer at the first two houses I tried, but at the third a woman in her thirties came to the door. She was wearing shorts and a T-shirt with headphones covering her ears. The cord ran down to the phone clipped to her belt.

"Hi, I'm Toni Lewis," she said after I'd introduced myself. "I bet you're here about those murders. I couldn't believe it. The world has gone crazy."

"I'd like to ask you a couple of questions about last night."

"Would you like to come in, or we could sit out here?" Toni indicated a couple of rockers on her porch.

"Out here is fine."

I scooted my rocker around so that I could face her. "Were you home last night?"

"Yes. I get home around six usually, a little earlier on Friday. TGIF as they say," she said lightheartedly, but then shook her head sadly. "Oh, I shouldn't be so callous when people have died."

I considered letting her know that the latest victim had been an actual creep and that the world might just be a better place without him in it, but I decided it was better to let her think he was an unfortunate victim.

"Did you see any odd cars or people who looked out of place?" Her house was just one block over from the spot where the car that Moreno had probably arrived in had been parked.

"I did, actually. I went out for a little walk right around dark. I do that sometimes. Occasionally, I even see a neighbor. Anyhow, I was going down the cross street and I heard someone cursing. I was a block away and the sun was already down, but there was just enough light for me to see a man standing beside a car parked at the curb. He seemed really frustrated. Like the way you get when your key won't work, or you keep fumbling with your purse." She paused and then laughed a little. "Of course you don't have a purse, but you know what I mean."

"What did the man look like?"

"I can't say. The light was fading fast, and he was hunched over trying to get the car door open. Or at least that's what he looked like he was doing."

"What about the car? Can you tell me anything about the car?"

"Jeez, let me think. Light-colored. I don't think it was white. Not new. Looked a bit dirty... maybe, but, like I said, the sun had gone down so it was hard to tell."

"Were you looking at the front of the car or the back?"

"The front."

"Did it have a plate of any type on the front bumper?"

She scrunched up her face. "Not that I remember."

"Did you see him get into the car?"

"Yes, well, almost. I saw him get the door open. He looked like he was trying to get in, but like it was difficult for him. I thought he might be physically challenged. Kinda felt weird watching him, so I started walking again."

"Did you see or hear anything else?"

"I thought I heard him start the car and drive away, but I was halfway down the next block by then so I didn't see him drive off. What I heard could have been another car."

I asked a couple more questions and got her number before giving her my card and telling her to call me if she thought of anything else. I appreciated getting her information, but it wasn't much to go on. You weren't going to inspire patrol officers by asking them to look out for a light-colored car that wasn't new and might be dirty.

The door at the next house was answered by a eight year-old, followed closely by a boy of about eleven who yelled for his mom at a decibel level that would have had OSHA recommending everyone in the house should wear hearing protection.

His mom came to the door looking like she'd been running a marathon.

"I don't know who you are, but if you could get the schools to have classes seven days a week, I'd be willing to give you all the money I have." From her tone and demeanor, I didn't think she was joking.

I explained who I was and why I was knocking on doors in the neighborhood.

"One of my co-workers mentioned that there had been a murder around here. Last night, though? That's odd because she mentioned it to me on Thursday," she said, looking puzzled, and I explained that there had actually been two murders.

"Damn! I guess I shouldn't be letting my kids answer the door." She looked genuinely shocked to discover that two murders had occurred only two blocks from where she lived.

I ran through my list of questions and got negatives. She hadn't heard or seen anything.

"Good Lord, we eat about that time. I wouldn't hear a bomb drop on my front yard when everyone's fighting over the chicken legs or who gets to put mustard on what."

"I appreciate your time," I said and started to leave after handing her a card.

"You know, now that I think about it, there was something."

I turned back. "What?"

"This was later. Maybe ten o'clock."

"Might still be important," I prodded.

"Hubby had finally gotten home, so I took the opportunity to leave the kids with him. I made up an excuse that I wanted to pick up some beer from the Fast Mart. I knew that beer was the magic word and he wouldn't mind watching the munchkins if I was going for something that important. What I really wanted to do was just cruise around in the car for a few minutes by myself."

"And you saw something when you were out driving?"

"Yeah, I guess it was a couple of blocks that way." She indicated a direction to the north. "I had the radio on and was having a good time when I noticed a car at an odd-as-hell angle. At first I thought he'd hit the telephone pole, but as I drove by I saw that he was just parked there. Drunk was what I thought at the time."

"What did the car look like?"

"It was an older Ford Fiesta. Light-colored, but it was hard to tell exactly what under the streetlight. Maybe white, possibly silver, maybe even a light grey. Had an Alabama tag and a bumper sticker for someone running for office. Nothing from around here."

"Where was this?"

"The street that runs behind the drugstore."

"Could you give a description of the man?"

"Nah, not really. The first time I saw him, he was just slumped over the wheel. Head down on his arms like…" She dropped her head and flopped her arms, demonstrating.

"You said the first time. When did you see him again?"

"I'm cursed with an imagination. I got to thinking when I was at the Fast Mart that maybe the guy was dying or something. You know, maybe he'd had a heart attack or low blood sugar. My mom had diabetes and she could get really foggy in her head when her sugar went down too low. So I decided to drive back by."

"What was he doing then?"

"At first I thought he was gone. 'Good,' I said to myself. 'I won't have to get involved.' But when I looked over at the back of the drugstore, I saw the car parked up close to the building and he was standing by the wall doing something. Taking a piss, maybe."

"What'd you do then?"

"He wasn't dead or dying so I went home."

I thanked her, then called Darlene as soon as I was back on the sidewalk. We met back at the car and rode over to the drugstore together.

We parked behind the store, approaching the area carefully in hopes that there might be some evidence in the area that we wouldn't want to disturb.

"Water spigot," Darlene said.

"He was trying to clean himself up."

The spigot was five feet from the back door of the drugstore. Of course, being behind the store and only thirty feet from the dumpster, there was litter and sticky grime on the ground. I went over to the dumpster and looked in. The odor of trash stewing in the warm air caused my stomach to roll over. There was no dead body, but there was a curious undertone to the usual scent of eau de dumpster.

Looking more closely, I saw a clump of clothes that appeared to have blood on them. Flies buzzed around the pile, creating a sickening humming sound.

"Got something!" I shouted to Darlene, who was looking up, trying to spot any security cameras.

We called Shantel, who quickly reminded us that she wasn't even supposed to be working today, but still agreed to come out with the van.

Half an hour later, the crime scene van pulled up with a patrol car right behind it. Deputy Julio Ortiz stepped out of the car.

"I recruited some good-looking help," Shantel told us.

"Now, now," Julio protested with a smile.

There were four items of clothing wrapped up in a ball. The middle of the bundle was still wet from water and blood. There were two old T-shirts, a pair of work pants and a towel. All of them had blood on them.

"He must have been messed up pretty bad," Julio said.

We did a sweep of the area, hoping that something might have fallen out of his pockets or out of the car. The only fresh things we found were a drink cup, a half empty Coke bottle, some cigarette butts and a few fast-food wrappers. The rest of the trash looked to have been out in the weather too long to be related to our case.

"I'm going back in to see if the manager has shown up." I'd walked into the store while we had been waiting on Shantel, but the day manager was pretty much useless. He wasn't willing to make any decisions, so I had talked him into calling his boss, who had promised to come in and assist us.

Walter Powell looked and acted just the way you'd think a manager of an old-fashioned drugstore would. He had short grey hair on top of a fatherly, mahogany-colored face. He was a few inches taller than me with slightly bent shoulders.

"Now what can I do for you? Always appreciate the quick response we get from you all. Thank goodness we haven't had any trouble here for a while," he said in a kindly manner.

"We think that a man who's wanted for questioning in a murder may have used the spigot at the back of your building to clean himself off last night."

"Really!" He sounded both surprised and curious.

"Do you have a security camera that covers the back of the building?"

He frowned. "We used to, but corporate hasn't gotten out here to fix it. They insist on handling all aspects of security, but then they let us go for six months without all of our cameras. I've had half a mind to email the lawyers and let them know the ball is being dropped. But then… I like my job," he said with an apologetic smile.

"I'd still like to look at whatever footage you have for last night between eight and midnight."

"Sure, come on back. I've got our regional security guy's number if we need anything. He's pretty responsive, even on a Saturday."

Just not responsive enough to get your dumpster camera fixed, I thought.

In the manager's office at the back of the store was a smaller room where the store's computer server and security monitors were located. Powell had to unlock the door. The room was cold, with the ten-by-ten space serviced by two air conditioner vents.

"Always cold in here. Got its own thermostat," Powell told me as he sat down in front of the monitors. "Guess cameras everywhere make your life a little easier."

"You'd think that, but they always seem to be pointed in the wrong direction or have too much grain or get erased…"

"Or they're broken. See your point, young man," he said while concentrating on the monitors. "Okay, here is the main parking lot." He pointed to the center screen. "I'll fast-forward. Let me know if you want to stop and take a closer

124

look at something."

Images flashed by, but not so fast that I couldn't see cars and people coming and going from the front parking spaces. We stopped half a dozen times when I saw a car or a person who looked interesting, but nothing panned out.

"Next I'll pull up the camera from inside the store facing the front door."

He started the recording and I saw mostly the same people coming and going.

"I think I'm seeing a few more people coming in than I saw in the first footage."

"That's right. Some people park on the side of the building and a few people walk up from behind and aren't caught by that front-facing camera. That's why we have this inside camera to catch everyone coming into or going out of our store."

He continued to fast-forward the footage. I stopped him when, at ten-forty according to the time stamp, a figure wearing a hoodie came into the store, looking unsteady on his feet.

"Back it up!" I told him, wanting to reach out and manipulate the video myself. The hooded figure scurried backward through the glass doors, then the image froze for a fraction of a second before the figure wobbled unsteadily through the door again. The person on screen set a can down on one of the displays inside the door and continued to move through the store.

"Follow him."

"Give me a second," Powell said. A different image popped up on the monitor, then whirled backward until I saw Hoodie come onto the screen. He looked around for a few seconds before moving directly toward the far wall of the store. The man had his back to the camera and was moving up and down along the wall. He would stop or squat down every couple of minutes. One time a clerk started in his direction and Hoodie moved away.

"Can we get a closer look at what he's doing on that

aisle?"

"Let's see." Powell worked some more magic with the system, rewarding us with a closer view but at an awkward angle. Even still, it was clear what Hoodie was doing. Powell actually growled a little. "Stealing. Nothing I hate worse than shoplifters. Bold as brass, some of them."

Hoodie seemed to have gotten what he wanted and started weaving his way back to the front of the store. At one point, he grabbed a bag of potato chips and wobbled up to the front counter. He talked to the clerk who was checking him out, waving his hands around as he did so. He paid for his chips, then snatched the bag out of the clerk's hand. He grabbed his can from the display on his way out the door.

"Back to the parking lot. See if we can tell where he went." Even as I spoke the words, Powell was already pulling the images up on the monitor. Nothing.

"He must have been hugging the side of the building," Powell said.

"Could you tell what he was stealing?"

"That wall is first aid. Didn't see exactly what it was he was pocketing, but we keep Band-Aids, bandages, antiseptics for cuts and abrasions, things like that along that wall."

Which made perfect sense. This was our guy. He'd gotten cleaned up enough so that he could come into the store, pretending to be a drunk homeless guy so that the clerks would mentally write him off, then steal the bandages and stuff that he needed to treat his wounds.

We spent half an hour trying to get the best close-up image that we could. Darlene came in at some point and I explained what we were looking at.

"Unfortunately there's no clear picture of his face. But look at this." I pointed to the one close-up image we'd managed to capture. The hood was pulled down, hiding his face from the camera, but it was possible to see the right side of his throat under his chin. A tattoo of a spider web spread up the side of his throat.

"Not a big surprise there," Darlene said.

"What's that mean?" Powell asked, pointing at the tattoo.

"Prison time. And it at least gives us one identifying mark. We're going to need to talk to the clerks that were on duty."

"No problem. I'll just give them a call. You want me to make a copy of all this?" He waved toward the monitor.

"Please."

"No problem." He was already punching a speed dial button on his phone. *Why can't everyone be as competent and helpful as Mr. Powell?* I wondered.

After two phone calls, he looked up at us. "Barry will be here in about twenty. He's the one who checked the man out at the register. Irene will be here in about an hour; she lives in Tallahassee. That was her that you saw approaching him on the video. I wouldn't be surprised if she just didn't want to deal with a homeless man. I don't really blame her, but I wish sometimes that she was more willing to confront problem customers."

Barry was a lanky, pimply kid in his early twenties.

"I remember him. Crazy homeless guy. I couldn't tell when he was talking to me and when he was talking to himself."

"Could you identify him if you saw him again?" Darlene asked.

He frowned. "No, not really. He kept his head down. Most of his face was hidden by the hoodie, which was filthy. He had some crazy tattoos on his neck and hands. I saw that."

Barry gave us the best description of the tattoos that he could remember. Definitely prison tats.

"He had a can with him that he set down over there." I pointed to the place that I'd seen the man leave the can in the security footage.

"I didn't see the can until he picked it up on the way out. Beer can of some sort. I can't really say what kind."

"Have the trash cans out front been emptied yet?" I

asked.

He shook his head.

Finished with Barry, Darlene and I went out front to sort through the trash as we waited for the other clerk. There was a chance the man had tossed the can after he no longer needed it for a prop.

"This guy isn't stupid," I said, picking through old receipts, fast food cups, napkins and other trash.

"Got a little bit of the actor in him, that's for sure. I've met some pretty cunning criminals."

"He sounds more like a fox than a hen."

"He's the one that survived the fight at the vet. Him *and* Sandra, apparently."

"Here, look at this." I lifted a can out of the trashcan with a pen, which I was never going to use again after this.

Darlene called Shantel, who came around and dusted the can for prints before sliding it into a plastic evidence bag.

"One good one and two partials," she said, handling the lifted prints carefully. "I'll scan them and check them when I get back to the office. You know you're paying me Saturday rates, right?" she kidded. "Julio and I are done out back. I'll call you if I get a hit on the prints."

The other clerk showed up just after Shantel left, but didn't have much to add to Barry's description. We thanked Walter Powell for his time, then Darlene called Deputy White.

"Find out anything interesting?" Darlene asked White over the phone. "We might have gotten a lead. Our man was at the drugstore... No, that's okay. It's all about the effort. Thanks." Looking at me, Darlene said, "Everyone was interested in the murder, but none of them saw anything."

"I'm feeling good about what we found here," I said, nodding toward the store. Looking at my watch, I saw that it was well past four. "I think we've done a good day's work. I'm going up to Columbus as soon as possible and see if I can track down more info on John Rybeck's background. See if I can tie him to Moreno."

Darlene gave me a salute for good luck and drove off. With a tired sigh, I followed her out of the lot, headed for home.

CHAPTER FIFTEEN

Once on the other side of my gate, I cruised up my driveway toward the house. I was greeted by the sight of my dad's van parked in front of the Laursens' yurt. *Just what I need*, I thought.

Before I could even get out of the car, Mauser came bounding around the side of the tent and threw himself against the car door. His tongue was lolling out of his mouth as he jumped up and down, waiting to give me one of his painfully joyous greetings. Reluctantly, I opened the door and took my punishment like a man.

"Okay, okay, that's enough. Where is your master?" I asked him, vigorously rubbing his ears. "Go get him!" I commanded. Mauser ignored me, continuing to lean against me and drool like a fire hydrant. "Fine, come on," I said, leading the way around the yurt. I could smell an oak campfire burning.

Sure enough, on the other side of the tent I found Dad, his girlfriend Genie Anderson, Henry and Anna sitting around a small fire. Various iron pots and skillets lay on or beside the brightly burning logs.

"There he is!" Dad said loudly as Mauser and I walked up. I couldn't be sure which of us he was referring to.

The front door of the house opened and Cara came out, carrying several bowls and silverware. She looked put-upon.

"I cooked up some peach cobbler in the Dutch oven," Anna told me as she gathered some of the bowls from Cara. I took the rest and gave Cara a greeting kiss. She smiled appreciatively.

"You look tired," she said to me.

"Are you sure you're not looking in a mirror?" I kidded her.

Genie and Dad were sitting next to each other on a couple of folding chairs that they must have brought with them. Mauser ignored both of them and went over to Henry, leaning back between his legs and letting the big man massage his head. They made quite the pair.

"I didn't know you all were coming," I said to Dad, trying not to sound as unenthusiastic as I felt about the situation.

"Henry wanted to see Mauser and invited us over."

He invited you over to my *house*, I thought, but immediately told myself to let it go. Actually, it was kind of nice to see all of the strange people in my life sitting around a campfire together. *If you can't beat 'em, join 'em*, I thought and pulled a lawn chair up to the fire.

After finishing a bowl of the best peach cobbler I'd ever eaten, I reached over and took Cara's hand. Her other hand petted Alvin, who was snoring lightly in her lap. The sun had gone down, leaving our faces lit by the flickering glow of the fire. Occasionally, the light breeze would cause a swirl of sparks to fly up from the fire, mixing with the stars in the sky. The warm night air was heavy with the scent of Confederate jasmine and the calls of a whip-poor-will echoed through the trees. For a moment I allowed myself to forget everything else and just enjoy the time spent with the important people in my life.

Dad was telling war stories from his early days as a deputy. He knew how to spin a good tale with little exaggeration. I'd seen him enthrall rooms full of old veterans and skeptical church ladies with equal skill. Once or twice, he and Henry butted heads over law enforcement policies and the rights of the people, but they kept it civil.

After a while, Henry asked, "Ted, who is this killer who's stalking the clinic?" Seeing Henry across the fire only increased his appearance to a throwback from the age of iron swords.

"Larry would have a better idea than me," Dad said and looked over at me. One reason that his deputies respected him so much was the fact that he would defer to them when it came to their own cases.

With everyone's eyes on me, I said, "Dad knows I can't say much about an ongoing investigation, but I think we picked up some good leads today. While the second murder and Sandra's disappearance are bad, they *have* provided us with a better idea of what might be behind the attacks."

I sounded more confident than I felt. It was true that we had more leads and that we were now sure that Sandra and the Columbus/Phenix City area were at the center of the investigation; however, we still didn't have a clear picture of motive or what role Sandra was playing. Drugs were a good guess, but a guess is not a fact.

"I just want to be sure that Cara is safe," Henry said, sending that father-of-the-daughter stare straight into my eyes.

"No more than I do."

"I'm sitting right here," Cara said. "I can take responsibility for my own safety. I'm not a child or someone who can't defend myself." She pulled her hand calmly away from mine.

Henry looked as if he was fighting the urge to roll his eyes. Instead, he stared at the ground for a second, then looked back at us. "Life can change in a moment. We all have to watch out for each other. That isn't weakness, but strength." He sounded like one of his ancestors giving a pep talk to the crew of a dragon boat. "I love you and you shouldn't be offended that I want to protect you."

"Kids never appreciate what a parent goes through," Dad said, sounding resigned.

"And vice versa," I couldn't resist lobbing back.

"True. I don't think my parents ever appreciated how much I did for them," Dad said thoughtfully.

As much as it made me uncomfortable seeing my dad with a girlfriend, I had to admit that his attitude had improved. With his re-election campaign in full throttle, it was a good time for Genie to have come along. Holding the office of sheriff was stressful enough, but with the added pressure of a contested election, anyone would have had a hard time keeping their mental and emotional equilibrium.

A little while later, I pulled Dad aside.

"I need to drive up to Columbus tomorrow."

"Background?" he asked curiously. While he grumbled about budgets, he wouldn't hold back when an investigation was at stake.

"More than that." I went on to explain all of the threads that led back to the Fort Benning area. "Even if the root causes aren't there, I think there are people who can shed light on the motives behind the murders."

"You need to go tomorrow?"

"Since it's Sunday, I won't be taking time away from the investigation here. Darzi's not doing the autopsy on Moreno until Monday."

"Federal reimbursement rates apply," he said, only half joking. "What kind of backup can you expect from the locals?"

"I haven't let anyone up there know I'm coming yet. We're supposed to hear from a DEA agent any time."

"Do you want to take Darlene or Pete?"

"No, but Cara wants to go along. She's concerned for Sandra." I glanced over at the group sitting around the campfire. I'd seen Cara look over at us a couple of times.

"Do you think that's a smart thing to do?"

"Henry does have a point. Someone has committed a series of violent crimes centered around the vet clinic.

Having her with me might be safer for her than leaving her here," I argued, even though I had my own doubts about taking Cara into an unknown situation.

"You can't take the department's car if you take her." Dad made a last-ditch argument against taking Cara along.

"We'll go in her car."

Dad looked at me closely. Whatever he saw in my face must have convinced him that I wasn't going to change my mind.

"Be careful," he said, gripping my shoulder. This was about as close as he got to a hug. I assured him that we wouldn't take any chances.

Dad and Genie left around ten after an hour of swapping stories with Henry and Anna about growing up in the sixties and seventies. Cara and I listened with amused smiles on our faces, amazed that they'd all survived to see us be born.

Afterward, as Cara and I stood at the sink washing dishes, I asked her if she still wanted to go to Columbus with me.

"Of course I do! I need a break from Dad." She lowered her eyes for a moment, then looked back at me. "And I'm not quite ready to let you go that far away on your own."

I squeezed her hand. I'd been proud of how well Cara had handled my recent brush with death, but she still had a few wobbly moments. She'd had reservations about my career at the start of our relationship, not the least of which were the inherent dangers of the job. Seeing me hooked up to wires and tubes in the ICU had definitely tested her limits. I wished that I could promise her that it would never happen again, but we both knew that wasn't possible.

She shrugged her shoulders, shaking off her dark thoughts. "Besides, I really like Sandra. I guess maybe I didn't actually *know* her, but I can't just pretend that we weren't friends. If I'm there, I might be able to do something to help her. Are you sure that she was involved in something illegal?"

"No," I said honestly. "We don't have any proof that she

was involved in the break-ins or the murders. But we do know that she lied about her background and took the job at the vet under false pretenses."

"That's so crazy. I didn't see anything that would have made me suspicious."

"Which is something else that makes me think that she has darker secrets in her past. Someone who's that good of a chameleon didn't start yesterday."

"I know. I just feel like I need to understand what was going on with her. I want to understand why I didn't see through her act." Cara sounded vulnerable.

"There are some people in this world who are capable of hiding their true nature from the rest of us." I pulled her to me.

She gently pushed against my chest so that she could look into my eyes. "I want the chance to confront her," Cara said, determined.

"I understand."

She gave me another hug.

Anna came in carrying another dish. "I think this is the last of them."

I took the dish from her and went back to the sink, leaving Cara to explain to her mother that we would be gone all day Sunday.

"We'll be back this evening," I told Henry the next morning as we stood in the yard by Cara's car. He was giving me the stink eye.

"You're going up to Columbus to talk to people."

"Yes. Exactly. Just to talk with a couple of people." We'd already gone over this several times.

"And you're sure it won't be dangerous?" he pressed, suspicious.

"I'm as sure as I can be. Most people don't want to mess with a deputy. We'll be fine," I said, trying to move around him to the car door. He didn't look like I'd convinced him.

"They'll be fine," Anna said to Henry, coming up beside

him and giving him a light punch on the arm. "Larry will take care of her. Quit hovering." To me she said, "We're going to work on getting a compost pile set up for you."

From her spot inside the car, Cara rolled her eyes and looked pointedly at her watch.

"That'll be great," I said to Anna, figuring anything that kept them busy was a good thing.

Heading north toward Columbus, I tried to make good time so that I'd have as much opportunity to question people as I could get. Cara was organizing a list of the names and numbers of the people I wanted to question. Most of them were contacts for John Rybeck that I had gotten from his parents or off of his phone.

"There's a lot of people here," Cara said, reviewing the list.

"Depending on what I find out today, I may have to come back up. But I didn't want to let a lot of time go by while Darlene and I weeded out the list. With Sandra in the wind, we need to act fast."

"So this trip is just a shot in the dark?"

"Exactly. Time is of the essence. Sometimes you have to balance the need to be thorough with the need to be fast. Right now, I think the need to be fast is winning."

The text alert went off on my phone. I handed it to Cara.

"It's from Darlene."

"I swear that woman never rests," I said, amazed. "What's she say?"

"She says she got an email from the DEA saying that they have an interest in the case. She told them that you were going to be in the Columbus area today and their agent wants to meet you there at noon."

Damn it! I had really wanted to get in and out of the Columbus area without having to get into an involved discussion about the case with other law enforcement agents.

"It's Sunday. What are people doing reading email and sending texts on a Sunday? They should be off enjoying the weekend," I grumbled as I realized the irony of this coming from me. "Fine. Tell her to text us where to meet him."

A few minutes later, I heard Cara give a small gasp. "Oh, that's not good."

"What?" I asked, trying to keep one eye on the road while glancing over to see what she was reacting to. Cara was staring at the phone. "What?" I repeated insistently.

"You aren't going to like this. The DEA agent is Matt Greene."

"Oh, hell," I said, willing it not to be true. Matt had been an investigator for Adams County until this past January. He and I had had several run-ins, including the last one where I'd arrested him. It had turned out to be one of my bigger screw-ups. We had parted on non-combative terms, but nothing friendlier. "Just my luck."

"You all were okay once the dust settled," Cara said, trying to mollify me. "And you always said he was a good investigator."

"He *was* good. No doubt about it. The problem was that Matt was never as good as he thought he was."

A childish part of me wanted to turn the car around and go home. Unfortunately, there was too much at stake. Getting some on-the-ground interviews done at the spot where all of our victims lives intersected was the best chance of aiding an investigation that could very easily ground out into a cold case.

"What should I tell her?" Cara asked.

Sighing, I said, "Tell her we'll meet him at high noon."

After responding to Darlene, Cara sorted through a few photos of Sandra that I'd brought along. It was high on my list of priorities to find out if any of Rybeck's friends knew Sandra. I had also obtained some not-dead photos of Moreno. With a history like his, there had been a wide variety of institutional portraits to choose from. If I could find someone who knew Sandra, Rybeck *and* Moreno, that would go a long way to figuring out what was at the center of this case.

"Do you really think that this is all about drugs?" Cara

asked.

"Very high odds. I doubt that Moreno has done much that didn't involve drugs since he got out of elementary school. I know that you have a hard time seeing Sandra as someone that would deal drugs, but you can't always tell by looking at someone."

"I know."

"Remember that some people become involved with drugs unwillingly. There are many cases where someone has been blackmailed or been threatened into smuggling drugs. Until we catch up to her or find someone who knows something and is willing to talk, we just won't know." I looked for a way to change the subject. "You know, your parents are really nuts."

"You'll get no argument about that from me," Cara said. Then she gave me a mischievous grin. "And your dad sure has a thing for Miss Genie. I saw them engaging in quite a bit of PDA last night."

"Stop. Please stop."

"He's not that old. He needs to have a little love interest," she said, poking my side.

"Hey, I'm trying to drive. I know and I'm not against it. Genie is a very nice person. But seeing my dad being all new-love-holding-hands-sappy-cute is too much."

Cara's poking was devolving into an attempt to tickle me.

"I'm driving. This is an official trip, and if you don't start acting responsibly, I'll have to leave you on the side of the road," I said, trying to hide my smile while avoiding her tickling fingers. "Enough!" I finally shouted.

"You're no fun."

We rode in comfortable silence for a little while before she asked, "Were you planning on trying to track down some of Moreno's drug contacts?"

"No. Not this trip. Maybe Matt will be able to fill us in on Moreno's connections. I never planned on pushing too deep into that on this trip. Even if you weren't along, I wouldn't fancy messing around in another jurisdiction's drug turf without knowing the players or the local rules."

"You make it sound like a game."

"It is a game. Very deadly, but a game. Hell, most of the players are under the age of twenty-five. These guys play until they're killed or placed permanently behind bars."

"Some people survive it and get out of the drug trade," Cara said, sounding more hopeful than convinced.

"A few. Maybe that's what Sandra was trying to do."

CHAPTER SIXTEEN

I wish I could say that I had mixed feelings about seeing Matt again, but the truth was that I really didn't want to have to deal with him. As soon as I saw him standing by his car in the parking lot, I knew that I wasn't going to enjoy this.

The lot was empty. Matt leaned against the hood of his car, arms crossed and looking judgmental. Sure enough, the first thing he did when we got out of the car was to ask why I'd brought Cara with me.

"She knows the person we're looking for. I thought she might be able to help."

"Fine. Let's go inside. Bring any pictures or information with you," Matt said as though speaking to a child.

"Great to see you too," I mumbled as I grabbed a file folder out of the car. I looked at Cara. "Mr. Charm is taking us inside the sanctum sanctorum."

Matt had a small office next to the FBI inside the SunTrust building downtown. Columbus isn't a large city.

"We've been working on a couple of supply lines. Let me see the pictures you have," Matt said, settling down in the chair behind his desk.

I handed him the picture of Sandra first. He looked at it hard. Matt was an ass, but he always took his job twice as seriously as anyone else. When he'd been a deputy and an investigator with our department, he'd rubbed a lot of people the wrong way, including me. But part of the reason he'd irritated so many colleagues was because he'd had his eye constantly on the ball, never taking time to smooth over hurt feelings or be one of the guys. On one hand, you had to admire that focus, but on the other, you had to ask yourself: would it have hurt him or his job performance to be a little more pleasant?

"No. I don't recognize her," he said after a minute. "But from what you tell me, she's been in Calhoun for a few years. I just joined the DEA a little while ago. Having said that, I've had time to go over the old files and I think I would recognize her. Honestly, there aren't that many women involved at the level of distribution that we're dealing with."

"I was wondering if she might have been a girlfriend or wife of someone involved," I said.

"These guys don't have long-term relationships. Even if they were inclined, it would be too dangerous for everyone. The creeps we're talking about use women like they're a disposable commodity. But I can take a picture and show it around."

I nodded, and as Matt took the picture with his phone, I got out the next photo.

"John Rybeck," I said, trading pictures with Matt.

"Rybeck I know. He's a strange one."

"He's a dead one," I told Matt, enjoying the fact that I could tell him something he didn't know. "John was our first victim. Killed by an overdose of animal tranquilizer."

"Self-administered?"

It wasn't that odd of a question considering that there are people who will use any drug available to get high. People huff paint, glue and even gasoline, let alone all the strange things that some are willing to inject, smoke or ingest. The desire to get high can be a primal drive.

"No. Someone stabbed him in the chest with a syringe

full of acepromazine."

"We had him listed as security."

"Security?"

"The bad guys around a drug operation can be put into categories—dealers, users, wannabes, security, workers and the abused."

"The abused?" Cara asked.

"Women who are used for sex, someone who's used as a mule, or just a family member unlucky enough to be stuck around these guys," Matt explained. "Sometimes workers also fall into the abused category. In a meth lab or wherever they are cutting drugs, the people working there can be doing it for the money or because they don't have any other choice."

"Why don't you just shut them down?" Cara asked.

"They leave them operating so they can follow the trail back up to the big guys. At least, that's the theory," I said cynically.

"That's not what we do," Matt insisted.

"Except when you want to drive up arrests. You just let it keep running so that you and the local police can arrest all the buyers and low-level dealers in an endless conveyer belt of stats."

This wasn't as uncommon as you'd like to believe. When arrest statistics equaled boasting rights and bigger budgets, there were plenty of unscrupulous law enforcement agencies that would take advantage of a drug operation that attracted drug addicts like bears to honey.

"We're on the trail of some major importers and providers here," Matt said, sounding irritated at my suggestion.

I held up my hand in a peaceful gesture. "I know. I didn't mean you in particular." I'd have liked to push more of his buttons, but we really did need his help. "What do you all know about Rybeck?"

Matt turned to his monitor and keyboard. After typing and scanning information for a while, he turned back to us.

"Rybeck worked for a mid-level distributor who runs drugs in a five-county area. He was first seen six months ago and was a semi-regular after that. One of the notes calls him a merci-be. That's a cross between a mercenary and a wannabe. Honestly, we don't have much interest in security. They are laterals who don't usually have any information about the guys higher up the food chain."

"That jives with the information we got from friends and relatives. The question is, why was he in Calhoun? I'm pretty sure that Sandra is part of the answer. What are her ties to the drug dealers?"

"We have a couple of informants that go back a few years. I can show her picture to them," Matt said.

"That would be great." Then I took out the picture of Moreno and handed it to Matt.

"This is one of the big guns. Him and a partner by the name of Erik Lopez. Lopez is the brains of the outfit. They work for a man we've marked as a prime target."

"So Lopez could be our second attacker?"

"Probably. They almost always work together." Matt printed out a photo of Lopez so that I could add it to my file.

"What's the name of the man they work for?"

Matt frowned. "I'm not going to give you that." He held up his hand, seeing my reaction. "It wouldn't do you any good. You can't waltz in and talk to this guy. In fact, most of the time I'd be hard pressed to tell you where you could find him. He travels almost constantly. And never without a number of guns around him.

"One of the reasons we haven't been able to take him down is that he owns nothing in the United States. Companies that he probably controls own lots of property, cars, phones and businesses, but everything leads to other people or to off-shore entities. Hard to get a warrant for a wiretap when the actual owners of everything appear clean and he's just a random visitor. He has enough places that he 'owns,'" Matt made air quotes above his head, "that for us to cover them all would take a sizable portion of our southeast agents."

"So you're telling me that I can't even question the man who employed my 'victim,'" I also made air quotes, "or his partner?"

"I'm saving you from yourself. This man and his operation have probably killed more people than you could count on your fingers and toes. There are at least two local law enforcement officers and a fish and wildlife officer that have been missing for years that he probably had a hand in. This guy has the use of several boats and at least three planes. If he wanted to get rid of someone, he wouldn't have that hard of a time getting rid of the body."

"People like that really exist?" Cara asked.

"They do. And they should be treated with the respect that you'd give a rabid grizzly bear. We *will* take him down, but at our last meeting on the subject we came to the conclusion that it's going to take a military operation to do it."

I could read between the lines of what Matt said. The DEA was seriously thinking about hitting this man when he was at sea or in the air.

"He's that bad?" I asked.

"I told you that Rybeck worked for an area distributor. The guy we're talking about is two levels above that. He is involved with most of the drugs that enter the country through the gulf ports," Matt said.

I felt my mind expand a bit to take that in. We were talking about an enormous level of income. I'm not a coward, but I suddenly had no interest in taking this guy on. I was actually glad that Matt hadn't given me his name. The less I knew, the better. Unfortunately, his men *were* involved in my case, with one of them now lying on a slab in the basement of a Tallahassee hospital.

"You've convinced me that I don't want to fool with this guy. So tell me, how can I investigate Moreno and his partner without attracting his attention?"

"I doubt that connection is important. Since Rybeck was working for the local guy, what I see happening is that Rybeck went down to Calhoun to try and fix a problem. He got dead. So the local guy asked the higher-ups for help. They sent Moreno and Lopez. So, really, the motive and the murders revolve around a local problem."

"Makes sense. I'm going to do some interviews while I'm in town." I paused and looked Matt squarely in the eye. "I'd appreciate it if you'd keep an ear to the ground."

"Of course. And I'll show the picture of the missing woman around too."

Cara and I started to leave when I had a thought. "We've got a partial description of the car that Moreno's buddy, possibly Lopez, was driving when he left Calhoun. Our witness saw an older, light-colored Ford Fiesta. They said it could have been white, silver or light grey with an Alabama tag and a political bumper sticker. Is there any way to check and see if that matches the description of a car associated with Moreno or Lopez?"

"We've been able to run a couple of surveillance operations since I've been here. They're labor intensive and, with only a couple of us permanently working the area, we can't do it as often as we'd like. But some good news—we've installed a couple of passive surveillance cameras." He turned back to his monitor, sounding excited. I'd never seen him that enthused before.

"Passive surveillance?"

"Automatic cameras that record all of the cars going to or coming from a location. We hide them in a derelict car. Leave it somewhere so that it points in the right direction, and it just logs every tag and snaps a picture. I can even monitor it from my phone. Luckily, drug operations frequently take place in locations where an abandoned car isn't unusual. Though we did have to stop an overzealous Phenix City police officer from having one of them towed away."

"Can you search the video?"

"The wonders of technology. I can search by tag, color, make, time of day and several other parameters."

I heard a printer running. "Check that out," Matt said.

I took the piece of paper he handed to me. Not only was there a photo of the back of a car showing the tag, but at the top was the registration information for the car. It belonged to a Mrs. Donald Price with an address in Phenix City. The car had been reported stolen two days ago. The timestamp on the screenshot indicated that the photo had been taken early Friday morning. Nothing unusual there. They had stolen the car with the intent of going down to Calhoun and doing their dirty deed. Total SOP for bad guys.

The only thing that I could do at this point was update the stolen car BOLO so that it included the information that the car was believed to be involved in a homicide in Adams County, Florida. The addendum would hopefully mean that when the car was located, the responding officers would have the good sense to call us before disturbing the evidence.

"With one of them injured, you might have a chance of finding the car," Matt said.

"If we get lucky."

He picked up his office phone and hit a speed dial button. "Columbus Police Department," he said, handing the phone to me.

I got in touch with a dispatcher who typed the information into the system so that, if the car was spotted, big red warning signs would go off. Not only was it important for our investigation, but any officer stopping or checking out the car needed to know that it had been involved in a violent crime.

Matt walked us out to the car.

"Good luck. Let me know if you need any more information. No guarantees, of course," he said and then added, "And try not to arrest me this time."

I almost fell over hearing a joke come out of his mouth. Even if it was a jab at me for screwing up and arresting him in an earlier case, he'd delivered it lightheartedly enough to make me believe that there might be a human being tucked beneath that self-righteous exterior.

We shook hands and parted on good terms. *Miracles do happen*, I thought.

"He was almost friendly," Cara said.

"I doubt it's that much fun being a DEA agent fighting a losing game with limited resources. Maybe he's remembering his days at the Adams County Sheriff's Office with a bit of nostalgia."

"Where to now?" Cara asked. I thought I detected some trepidation.

"Are you sure you don't want me to drop you off at a restaurant? Or we could even get a hotel room. You don't have to go with me."

"No. I want to. I just got a little freaked out by all that talk about powerful drug lords. It's like something out of a movie."

"Those people and organizations do exist. And it *is* scary. What's really terrifying is that those organizations' revenues are so huge that they can buy people in powerful positions."

"Great, so not only are you dealing with people who would kill you on a whim, but they have the clout to get away with it."

"Exactly. And if they can't buy someone, then they'll try and blackmail or threaten them or their families to get what they want. That's what an income of hundreds of millions of dollars and no morals can do."

"Promise me we'll stay out of their way."

"It would be tantamount to suicide for me to try and go up against them. Like a squirrel stepping in front of a locomotive and sticking his little paw up. They wouldn't even feel it when they plowed me into the ground. I can promise without hesitation that I won't go anywhere near them."

"Thanks. That makes me feel better."

"And, to answer your question, we're going to Rybeck's

apartment and then to talk to his friend Duke." I handed her my phone. "His address is in my text messages."

CHAPTER SEVENTEEN

Rybeck's apartment was one of four in a concrete block building that sat on the edge of a large parking lot with several others just like it. I parked in front of the building that had an office sign hanging from one door.

My knock was answered by a small, tough-looking old man with grey hair cut short and tanned, leathery skin. He stood and moved like the ex-military man that he was. He told me that his name was Clayton and he owned the complex.

"John. Nice kid. Going to get into trouble, that was clear. If I'd had him in boot camp, I could have made a hell of a soldier out of him."

"Why did you think he was going to get into trouble?"

"He was looking for someone to model himself after. He was looking for a hero. I seen lots of kids like that come into the Army. We give them heroes. Problem is that a kid like John wants adrenaline, wants that rush. In the Army," he shrugged, "well, we can give them all the excitement they want, but it's mixed with discipline. Out here," he waved a hand, "adrenaline usually means trouble. When John couldn't get in the military, he started hanging around bad people. Of course, some of them were men from the base who were trouble in their own right. Rotten little shits that just haven't been caught and kicked out yet."

"Caught for what?"

"Whatever trouble they get into. Always some bad apples that haven't gotten tossed out of the barrel." He looked like he knew how to deal with bad apples. "I had to tell more than one of them that I didn't want them hanging around here. Had a couple bow up at me. That's all right." He lifted his shirt and showed me a Colt Commander in a holster tucked inside his pants. "Don't worry, I got a carry permit."

We had been walking while he talked and were now standing at the door to Rybeck's apartment. He unlocked the door and stood back, letting me enter. I put on a pair of latex gloves and turned on the light. Even with the light on, the room was dark. The shades were drawn and one of the two bulbs in the overhead light was burned out.

I didn't want to disturb anything, not even the blinds, so I took out my flashlight to help me look around. The living room was a typical young man's bachelor hovel, complete with the classic scattered pizza boxes and beer cans. The walls, however, were covered with posters featuring the Army, Marines and various action heroes. In one corner was a small collection of various fantasy swords. The TV was hooked up to a PlayStation that looked well used. The small, open kitchen featured several liquor bottles on the counter, along with a half empty canister of some sort of protein mix. The cabinets were bare and the refrigerator held only fast-food leftovers and a plastic bottle of milk that had clearly gone over.

There was only one bedroom. In it was a queen mattress on a metal frame. A few condom wrappers were in the wastebasket. The posters in here were of scantily clad, buxom women being defended by various Conan the Barbarian imitators. Some of the Conan stand-ins were carrying guns or laser blasters instead of swords, but those and the damsels' hair colors were the only differences. The only interesting thing I found was some pot in one of his drawers and a syringe bottle that might have held steroids. Nothing indicated that anything had been wrong when Rybeck last left the apartment.

Going back outside, I let Clayton lock the door before I pulled out the pictures of Sandra, Moreno and Lopez.

"I don't recognize any of them. Though those two are cut from the same cloth as some of the ones that come around here causing trouble."

I thanked Clayton and told him that I wanted to keep the apartment locked down for a few more days at least.

I checked in on Cara, who was sitting in the car reading a book, and I told her I was going to go see Duke Waters. After how he had gone on about pretty girls, I felt like I was cheating him by not encouraging Cara to come with me.

Duke's apartment was in the building next to Rybeck's. It took the old man a while to get to the door. At least three times he shouted that he was coming and for me to hold my horses. When the door did open, he was sitting in a wheelchair with an oxygen bottle strapped to its side and a plastic tube running up to his nose.

He invited me in and I closed the door behind me. In contrast to Rybeck's apartment, Duke's was uncluttered and bright, with all of the curtains and windows open. There was a slight smell of old age and illness in the air.

"I still can't get it into my head that he's dead. Why the good ones? Never understood that. I'm going to give God hell about it when I see him. Preachers can talk all they want about a mysterious plan, but it still doesn't ring fair." His voice was surprisingly strong and his eyes were hard as flint.

"I've got some pictures I'd like you to take a look at," I said, showing him all three photos.

"Nope. Haven't seen none of them," Duke said.

We talked for a while, partly because I felt guilty for having disturbed him, but he didn't have anything else to add to what he'd said on the phone.

"Nothing," I said in answer to Cara's question about how things had gone. "Odd that these four people are tied together by the circumstances of their deaths or disappearances, but they don't seem to have any other connections."

"Of course, Matt made it sound like Moreno and Lopez were brought in after Rybeck's death," Cara said.

"True. But you'd think that there would be some tie to Sandra. It would help if we could find her," I said and saw the pained look on Cara's face. I put my hand on her knee. "We will."

"You can't promise that."

"No fair calling me out when I'm trying to comfort you," I said and got a small smile in return. I leaned over and she let me give her a quick kiss.

Then my text alert went off with a message from Rybeck's friend Cherry. I'd tried calling her, but she hadn't answered or returned my calls, so I'd resorted to a text with a mild threat that involved more visits from the local PD. She was finally texting back that she'd meet me at a Waffle House in half an hour.

We Google-mapped our way to the restaurant and found Cherry sitting at a table near the door, nursing a cup of coffee and looking nervous. It was one o'clock and she looked like she'd just woken up. Night work.

Cara sat down in the booth beside me. I wasn't sure if it would help or hurt having a woman along, but I already knew what Cherry's opinion was of me, so I figured having Cara along couldn't hurt.

"Great to finally meet you in person," I said with a smile, knowing that I was probably pushing her buttons a little but unable to stop myself.

"Eff you," she said. "You a cop too?" she asked Cara.

"No. Just along for the ride."

"Good for you."

We went over the basics again and her story stayed consistent.

"I'm just really freaked out over him getting killed," she said.

"If you know anything that could be helpful, I'd suggest you tell me. Right now I don't have a good handle on a motive, which means that I can't tell you if you're in danger or not. Any information that you can give me could clear the muddy waters a little." I pulled out the pictures. "Have you seen any of these people?"

"What, like in real life?" she said in an odd way that made me wonder what she meant.

"Why did you say it like that?"

"Because I haven't seen them, like really seen them, but I've seen this picture before," she said, tapping the one of Sandra. My heart beat faster. Was I really going to get a lead?

"Where and when did you see this picture?"

"John had a copy of it in his car the last time I saw him. He had said that he might be gone a day or two and I'd noticed an envelope in the seat with a piece of paper sticking out of it. When he went into a store to get some beer, I pulled the paper out a little to look at it. It was a copy of this picture, only a little smaller, but definitely the same one. There were a couple of addresses in Florida and another picture or two of buildings. Some stuff was highlighted in yellow."

"What was highlighted?"

"Dates and stuff. Didn't make much sense to me."

"What else was in the envelope?" Cara asked, surprising me.

"Nothing," Cherry said in an obvious lie.

"Come on, what?"

"Some money," Cherry finally said, looking upset.

"What's wrong?" I asked.

She just stared down at the table.

"How much did you take?" Cara asked.

"There were a bunch of hundreds. I just took one. I feel really shitty about it."

"Can you take a guess how many more there were?" I asked.

"Maybe fifty?" she said. "I kinda thought that's why you

were calling that first time. Maybe he'd reported me. Made sense why I hadn't heard from him. Then, when you told me he was dead, it got in my head that I might have caused it somehow by taking that money."

"I don't think his death had anything to do with the missing hundred dollars," I told her. That much was the truth; however, I was also pretty sure that his death had everything to do with that envelope and the money inside of it.

"That's good. I thought, like, maybe some creeped-out drug dealers had found out the money was short and killed him because of it." Cherry clearly had a conscience and an over active imagination.

"Did he say anything about the picture or the money?" I asked.

"No. I acted like I didn't see it and we never talked about it."

We went over everything else that she could remember about the last time she had seen him. I'm sure that if she'd known it was going to be the last time, she would have committed more to memory. But, she said that the meeting was not much different than dozens of others they'd had.

When Cara and I were back in the car, I told her how impressed I was that she had ferreted out the fact that Cherry had looked in the envelope and stolen the money.

"Elementary," she said with a slight smile. "Really, just curiosity. I know I couldn't have resisted looking. As for the money, Cherry might as well have had 'desperation' tattooed on her forehead. Sad. I think she's a nice girl at heart, but I can't help thinking that something bad is going to happen to her."

"Something bad happens to most people," I said, and then went on, "Sorry, I know what you mean. But you can't tell. I've seen folks who were further down than she is end up on their feet. She's young. She has time if it isn't stolen from her," I said, putting the car in gear.

I'd pretty much exhausted my leads, but at least I'd

gotten some insight into Rybeck and had confirmed that he was being paid for something related to Sandra. I didn't have time to go diving into the local drug world. I'd wait until I got more intel from Matt. I'd hoped to talk with more people who had known Rybeck, but the meeting with Matt had taken up some of our time. Dad was going to love more back-and-forth to Columbus.

"What do you think he was being paid for?" Cara asked.

"Good question. A hit? That seems unlikely. He doesn't seem the sort. Now Moreno and Lopez, on the other hand, are certainly the right type."

"Could have been that someone took a chance on him. Thought they could get it done cheap," Cara said.

"Maybe."

"You don't sound convinced."

"He just seems too... nice. But he might have taken the job for some reason that we haven't figured out. If the money wasn't for a hit, maybe he was supposed to deliver it to her. Or he was just supposed to rough her up."

We stopped at a barbeque joint in a small town in Georgia for a late lunch. I had just finished my ribs and was trying to wipe all of the sauce off of my fingers when my phone rang. It was Marti in dispatch.

"Got what you've been waiting for. The suspect's car from the clinic murder has been called in. It's just north of the Georgia line." He gave me the location and general directions. It seemed pretty clear that the suspect had been heading back toward Columbus.

Cara quickly paid the bill while I headed for the car. "I'm on my way," I said. "I should be there in about forty-five minutes."

"You'll like this. The trooper reports that there is a trail of blood leading away from the car. He followed it for about a hundred feet and then decided that he needed to stay with the car. I gave him—"

I cut Marti off when my phone started to buzz with another call. I glanced at the ID and saw that it was a

Georgia number. "I think he's calling now." I hung up on Marti and answered the incoming call as I pulled out of the parking lot. Trooper Freeman introduced himself and I told him that I'd already gotten a call about the car.

"It's parked back down a dirt road. Got reported by some kids on an ATV. What do you want me to do? The blood's not fresh. I've called one of our county investigators. He should be here in a few minutes."

"If you can preserve the scene, that would be great. I'm inbound and should arrive in thirty-five minutes or so," I said, laying my foot down a little heavier on the gas pedal.

"Roger that."

Cara and I found the site after a couple of questionable turns. The car was almost hidden up a dirt path that was meant more for four-wheelers. I got out and introduced myself to Trooper Freeman and Lt. Wayne Rogers.

"So we got a stolen car," Rogers said. He couldn't have been more than a couple of years from collecting social security, but his eyes were sharp. "You said there was blood?" he said to the trooper, a small guy who looked a bit lost in his hat.

"Over here."

We approached the car as carefully as we could, and Freeman pointed out some darker-colored mud in the clay. Looking past the car, I could see a couple more areas that were similar. "I followed them for a while, but decided that I should call it all in. Besides, it's dried up. I yelled and didn't hear anything."

"Okay. One of us should go down the path as far as we can and see if we find anything else," Rogers said.

There was so much undergrowth off of the path that there wasn't a choice. Whoever followed it would be disturbing the ground and any evidence, regardless of how careful they were.

"I'll go, if you don't mind," I said.

Rogers nodded. "Seems like this is part of your case anyway."

I took out my phone, turned on the video and let it lead me down the path. If I was going to disturb the scene, at least there would be a record of what it looked like before I trampled all over it.

I could see what had to have been Freeman's shoeprints as I walked. Twenty feet past the point where he'd turned around, I saw a body lying next to a palmetto bush. I'd found Eric Lopez. But I wasn't the first person to find him. In the back of his head was a hole and in the front was a larger one where his nose should have been.

CHAPTER EIGHTEEN

Rogers had been polite, but he made it clear that he was in charge of the crime scene. I watched their techs and tried to determine how competent they were. The evidence and the body were handled professionally. Once his crew got started, Rogers and I moved off and talked about the case.

"So he and this other fella were trying to ambush some woman who worked at a veterinary clinic?" Rogers asked me. We were leaning up against his unmarked car as we talked.

"Exactly. And there was an earlier murder that also appears connected to the attack."

"You're thinking the woman killed the first guy with her car and stabbed this rascal with something. So do you think she somehow managed to find him and shoot him?" He sounded skeptical.

"I think there are other people involved. Drugs are part of this too. I can't see our missing woman doing this. However, I can't rule anything out at this point."

"We know he was shot in the car," Rogers said. That fact had been obvious when we observed that there was an unhealthy amount of brain tissue and blood in the car. Whoever had killed him had dragged him down the path and then done a half-ass job of trying to clean off the car window. I suspected they were just hoping to make it a little less obvious that there was blood all over the car.

"Found the bullet, Ace!" one of his deputies shouted over to us.

"Ace?" I asked. Rogers smiled shyly.

"Stupid nickname. Got it when I was first on patrol. I was lucky a couple of times, so they started saying I always had an ace up my sleeve. Honestly, looking back, I was foolish for getting into scrapes where I needed luck to get out of 'em." He put his foot up on the bumper of his car and pulled up his pant leg. "They gave me this for my twenty-fifth." The Colt snub-nosed revolver strapped to his ankle had pearl-handled grips with an ace of spades inlaid in black.

"Nice!" I said, liking the veteran investigator and hoping that he was as sharp as he was experienced.

"Don't worry," he said, apparently reading my thoughts. "We'll get the evidence and I'm not some turf-guarding idiot. I'm glad you're here. Means I don't have to start from scratch."

I excused myself and called Darlene.

"Let me guess, he still isn't talking," Darlene joked.

"No, the hole in his head seems to be hindering my interrogation of the suspect."

"Keep at it. You just haven't found his soft spot yet."

"Okay, enough," I said, feeling my stomach turn a little at her joke. "If you'd seen the body, you wouldn't be kidding about soft spots."

"I've spent my day collecting fingerprints at Sandra's house. I found a couple of sets that I'm pretty sure are hers. I also got some hair with the follicles still intact for a DNA sample. Marcus came in this afternoon to prepare the prints. We should know pretty shortly if there is a match in the NCIC. If not, we can try some of the other databases."

"You'd think there would be a good chance of a hit, considering the fact that this is someone who is being chased by hardened criminals and was capable of generating a new identity and hiding the old one."

"I hear you. One way or the other, at least we've got the DNA in case we find a body that needs to be identified." Darlene was practical and thorough. "And, just to be sure, I emailed the U.S. Marshals in case she was in the witness protection program."

"If she is, they aren't doing a very good job of protecting her."

"Maybe she wasn't a very good witness," Darlene said dryly and hung up.

I went back to check on the efforts to retrieve evidence from the car. It was a mess. The culprit's efforts to clean off the windshield had done little more than smear the tissue and blood around. The backseat held several bags from fast-food joints and various quicky marts. Bloody clothes were scattered around the car, along with wrappers from the stuff that Lopez had stolen from the drugstore. Inside the pocket of a pair of jeans we found a folded-up piece of paper. It was a print-out with a picture of Sandra and the addresses of both her house and the clinic.

I watched as Rogers's forensic team bagged and tagged everything. He let me take pictures of several items, including the note. I also emailed him the video that I'd shot walking back to the body. We shook hands and promised to talk soon.

Before we left, I did my duty by calling Matt and letting him know that he could cross Lopez off of his list of local operatives. I also let him know that we hoped to have the real identity of "Sandra" soon.

"Who was she? I just can't get past that," Cara said. She sounded tired and frustrated.

"Hopefully, we'll get a hit off the NCIC."

"That just seems worse. It'll mean she has a record."

"Not everyone that has a record is a bad person," I tried to console her.

"I know. I'm just used to people being open about who they are."

"I'm afraid you just haven't seen how much people hide about themselves. Admittedly, Sandra is an extreme case. But most people hide some part of themselves from the rest of the world. I can remember experiencing some of the same disillusionment you're feeling during my first couple of years as a deputy. I hadn't realized how complex and hidden some people's lives can be. It sort of distorts your worldview."

I took my eyes off of the road and glanced over to see Cara looking at me with narrowed eyes.

"Not that *I'm* hiding anything," I said with a smile. "At least nothing too terrible."

"Just so long as our relationship doesn't end like some gothic novel with me running away from your house in the moonlight, wearing my nightgown, after having discovered some dark secret in a closet," she said, some of her natural good humor returning.

"If that happens, it would only be because it's Ivy who's chased you away," I chuckled, imagining my tabby cat in the role of the evil lord of the castle.

When we got home we were greeted in the front yard by Mauser.

"What are you doing here?" I asked the Dane, who was busy rubbing his head against my legs and drooling.

"I asked your dad to let him stay over," Henry told me as he came out of the yurt wearing jeans and a linen—hell, it may have been hemp—shirt. "Thought with all the attacks it might be good to have the added protection."

Ha! I thought. Mauser was cut from the same cloth as Scooby-Doo when it came to bravery, and Henry the axe-wielding Viking hippy was perfectly able to defend himself. He didn't fool me one bit. He just liked having the big goofy dog around.

Cara and I were both tired and headed into the house, where we were greeted by the smell of onions and garlic.

"I thought you all would be ready for a warm meal when you got home," Anna said as she puttered around in the kitchen. She had the avid attention of both Alvin and Ivy.

Clearly, she'd been dishing out treats all day. Neither of the little turncoats gave us more than a glance as we went into our bedroom to freshen up.

My phone rang as I finished changing clothes.

"We got a hit on the fingerprints," Darlene said without preamble, then paused dramatically.

"And the winner is?" I asked a little irritably after a full day and yet another body.

"Kate Kelly. No middle name. She was picked up a few time in her early twenties for various misdemeanors. Possession, public intoxication, resisting arrest, nothing more serious. I'd have you guess her last known address, but you're clearly not in the mood for games. She was living in Columbus four years ago."

"I'm in a better mood already," I said, seeing Cara give me a quizzical look as she came out of the bathroom.

"I've updated the BOLO and I've sent out requests to get the arrest reports."

"Good idea. They'll mention any other people who were arrested at the same time and possibly give us a start on a list of known associates. We'll see what tomorrow brings. Are you done working for today? You do know that today is Sunday?"

"You're one to talk. You used the day to go dig up another body for us. If you could have caught that guy alive, it would have been a lot more useful."

"I was a few hours late, sorry."

"Do better next time, rookie."

After I hung up, I filled Cara in on Sandra's real identity as we went back into the kitchen.

"That's sooo odd," she said.

"You don't know all the facts yet," Anna said. She was putting the finishing touches on our dinner and, apparently, listening in on our conversation.

"Your mom's right. Maybe Sandra had good reasons for her actions." What do you say to someone who's just learned that a friend and colleague has been hiding their real life story?

"I know. I just feel like I've lost a friend. Even if I understand why she did it, the person I knew and worked with doesn't exist anymore."

I could see tears of frustration pooling in her eyes. I pulled her to me and let her wipe them against my shoulder. Then she pushed back away from me and said, "I'm okay."

"I'm going to do my best to find her. That's the only way to get to the bottom of this."

"And I want to help her. Up to the point that she's out of danger, and then I'm going to be really angry with her." Cara tried to joke, but her eyes couldn't smile.

"I'll leave you two alone now," Anna said. A faint smell of incense, and probably pot, followed in her wake as she went out the front door.

After dinner we spent a few hours vegetating with social media and light reading before I joined Cara for Alvin's bedtime walk. As we wandered across the yard we heard a deep-throated *woof* from the yurt as Mauser did his duty, alerting his current best friends to the intruders. But he wasn't going to over-exert himself that late at night and the one grumbly bark was all we got.

I thought how lucky Henry was that we were enjoying a particularly mild spring. Usually by this time of year Mauser would've become a worshipper of air conditioning, and you'd barely be able to encourage him to leave the house even to do his business. Spending the night in a tent would have definitely been out of the question. But tonight, by the time we went back into the house, I could hear at least two sets of snores coming from the yurt.

I got into the office before eight on Monday morning. There were leads to follow up on and I wanted to end this craziness for Cara and everyone else at the clinic.

"What news?" Darlene asked as she walked in.

"No words of praise for being here bright and early?" I kidded her.

"Do it five days in a row and I'll be impressed," she said, setting a bag from the Donut Hole down on my desk. "I thought that with your all-natural, possible-future in-laws staying at your place, you might need a good dose of sugar and fat."

"Cheers," I saluted her before taking a healthy bite of a chocolate-iced donut.

After we'd both settled in and checked our emails, we huddled around Darlene's desk to come up with a plan for the day.

"Do we need to attend the autopsy?" I asked.

"One of us should. Not that Darzi needs us looking over his shoulder, but since we're still very much in the dark as to what happened at the scene, we might be able to ask some good questions."

I flipped a penny. "Call it."

"Heads," Darlene said. The Lincoln Memorial greeted our eyes.

"Tell Darzi hi," I said. "Now that we have a new name for Sandra, I want to do a records search. See if we come up with any other cars or property. I'll also call Matt and see if he's got anything for us."

"You and Matt getting along these days?"

"We managed to be in the same room without getting into a knock-down fight."

"Good thing for you," she said snidely.

"You and the horse you rode in on. I'll check in with the folks in Georgia and make sure that the Lopez investigation is moving forward."

After Darlene had left for the autopsy, I spent some time making my phone calls. Rogers told me that they had found the bullet that had killed Lopez inside the car.

"Looks like we're going to be in luck. It went through his head and lodged in the foam of the car seat, so the bullet's in pretty good shape. We should be able to match it up to the gun if we find it. Still haven't found the casing. I think it's there, but the problem is that the ground is so sandy on that road it's hard as hell to find. I've got a couple of rookies out there shifting through the dirt looking for it. Autopsy will be this afternoon. I'll have our medical examiner pay special attention to the knife wounds. Our doc is pretty good with edged weapons."

I thanked him, then called Matt.

"I've got meetings set up with two of my CIs today. I'll call you when I know something," he told me curtly but professionally.

I thought about trying to do the public records search myself, but decided instead to use Beth Miller's professional help.

I walked down to the records office and saw that there were already three people in line. Beth was busy pulling copies of accident and incident reports. I should have thought about how busy Monday would be. Guiltily, I snuck in through the side door and waited patiently as she hustled back and forth until she finally got a break and turned to me.

Beth was in her forties and had worked for several different county departments before moving to the sheriff's office a dozen years earlier. Her clerical skills were surpassed only by her skill in the kitchen. She would always bring the best baked goods for special occasions, or just when she was in the mood to see how fast a Bundt pan of monkey bread could disappear. There was speculation that Beth actually worked for the company that made our duty belts and that her mission was to get us to gain weight so we constantly had to buy new belts.

"Macklin, I don't know what you're hanging around here for. I didn't bring any treats in today."

"It's your other talents I'm after," I told her, handing her a request for information sheet on Sandra, AKA Kate Kelly.

"Records then?"

"Yes, and you might check variations on her names. Mix and match them."

"You know, there is this thing called a computer?"

"I know. But I also know our county clerk runs about a

year behind on posting information to their website."

"There's a reason I left there and came to work over here."

"But you still have friends there," I said delicately.

"I'll get to it at lunch."

"I'll owe you."

"Unfortunately, you don't have enough pull with your dad to get me a raise."

"Sorry," I said and she laughed it off, walking over to help an elderly gentleman who'd wandered up to the counter looking confused.

I passed Pete on the way back to my desk. He barely noticed me.

"Hey, big guy. Why are you so lost in thought?" I asked

"I met with Mary this morning," he answered, causing me to stop and stare at him. Mary was the daughter of the man who had owned the town's favorite restaurant, Winston's Grill, up until the point that he was discovered to be a vicious serial killer. He'd pleaded guilty in return for multiple life sentences, so there had been no trial and Mary was no longer considered a witness. Pete wasn't breaking any ethical code by talking with her, but it was still odd.

"Why?" I asked, unable to hide my surprise.

"She wants to open another restaurant in town," he said hesitantly.

"That seems like a risk for her. Why'd she want to talk to you?"

Pete shrugged. "She said I was the type of patron she'd need if the restaurant is going to be successful." This was true. Winston's had been the main gathering spot for locals looking for generous portions of both food and gossip. Pete had been a regular.

"Why not open one somewhere else? She's going to have an uphill battle around here. A lot of folks felt betrayed when it came out that her father had been using the restaurant as a stalking field."

"And I was one of the angriest," Pete admitted. "But I

know she wasn't involved. And I think she feels that if she left town to start over, she'd always have the bad memories hanging over her. She wants to start fresh here, as her own person. Listening to her, I was pretty impressed with her attitude."

"What'd you tell her?"

"I said I'd have to think about it. I admire her gumption, but I'm not sure that she wouldn't just be setting herself up for a big fall. I told her that."

"What'd she say?"

"She thinks she'd be better off, even if she failed. Thinks it would get a lot of things out in the open and give her a chance to confront her ghosts. Those are her words."

"We all have ghosts. Hers are pretty big. Personally, I'd run from them."

"One part of me wants to tell her to move on, but part wants to encourage the courage."

"That second part is your stomach. You haven't been happy since Winston's closed."

"Sarah isn't a morning person and I'm not a cook. Besides, I miss the gossip. I swear it's twice as hard to dig up a lead without the loose lips at Winston's morning buffet."

"Speaking of which, don't you have some official work to do?" I chided him.

"A drive-by shooting and the victim won't tell me who did it, even though he knows. Plus a couple of battery cases. Nothing as interesting as yours. Any luck?"

I filled him in on how I'd spent my weekend.

"You could always bring in the FBI since there's a case to be made that this involves... well, something that took place across state lines."

"We tried that. Plus I have enough federal help with Matt."

"Big DEA guy. Glad I don't have to deal with him."

"He isn't being that bad. I think moving up to a bigger pond has deflated his big fish ego."

"It could use some deflating."

The text alert on my phone went off. Pete waved and headed for his desk, swiping the second donut that Darlene had brought for me as he passed mine. The text was from Eddie: *Got a hit on the photos. Meet me in half an hour.*

CHAPTER NINETEEN

I was shocked to hear from Eddie before noon. I tried to remember if that had ever happened before. Maybe he really was clinging to the sobriety bandwagon.

I met him at our usual spot in Rose Hill Cemetery. The sun was warm and we stood in the shade of a sycamore tree against the back wall.

"You found out something?"

"It isn't easy," he said, no doubt trying to bargain up the price of the information, "coming up with stories that sound plausible. But, yes, I did find a girl who admitted to seeing them."

"Which ones?"

"These." He pulled up the pictures of Moreno and Lopez on his phone. I'd forwarded Lopez's photo to him on Sunday.

"What did you tell her?"

"I said a dealer was looking for them. She was pretty burned out. Really, I shouldn't even be hanging out with her type. Very methy."

"I remember you having some methy moments yourself."

"I got my two-month chip." He pulled an AA chip from his pocket.

"Proud of you," I said, trying not to sound cynical. I kind of liked Eddie and I was glad he was staying clean.

"Yeah. I'll just be glad when the trial is over." Most of Eddie's family had been busted for an array of drug charges and he had helped to bring them down. He was justifiably nervous about testifying against them.

"So what did she remember?"

"She said that they'd stopped by her dealer-slash-pimp's house looking for something."

"What?"

"She wasn't real clear."

"When was this?"

"Maybe Saturday? Though it could have been Friday. She stays pretty fried."

"I get that. What *does* she remember?"

"She said they were really bossy. Her dealer was trying hard to help them. I know the guy and he's never helpful. She did hear them say that this was about a big score."

"A big score? What about a big score?"

Eddie pulled out his phone and pressed something. A voice as grating as shards of glass on a chalkboard broke the stillness of the cemetery.

"I recorded her," Eddie said proudly. He fiddled with his phone a bit, advancing the recording. "Here."

"They were creepy as shit and pushy," the woman's voice slurred. *"Hey, whatcha got for me? Gimme somthin'."*

"Later. What else happened while the men were there?" Eddie said on the recording.

"I don't know. My head hurts. I gotta get me somthin'." She sounded like she was falling asleep.

"It was just the four of you at the house?"

"Yeah." There was some dead air. *"Until the other asshole got there."*

My ears perked up.

"Who showed up?" Eddie asked. I had to hand it to him— he was doing a good job of questioning her.

"The one... all hyped up. Told them they had to do it the way he

had it planned out. Som' such shit."

"What did he look like?"

"An asshole," she said, sounding proud of her descriptive powers.

"Tall?"

"Everybody is tall to me, honey. Now gimme a little."

"What color was his hair?"

"You sure ask a lot of questions?"

"I told you, there's a guy who wants to know. This could be good for all of us."

"I can't mess with my hook-up." She sounded panicked.

"No, this guy is big. We make him happy, you'll never have to worry about the next hit."

"Oh, man, wouldn't that be great?" You could hear her drifting off into a drug-induced fantasy land of unlimited highs.

"But we got to help him. Just tell me what this asshole looked like."

"Yeah, alrigh'. Tall, I guess, blonde, large ears, short hair. How 'bout that?"

"What was he wearing?"

"How the fu... I don' know. Clothes. Kinda work clothes."

"Business clothes?" It sounded like Eddie was having to shake her to keep her awake.

"No, no, like a guy who works for a livin'. Blue! Yeah, they were blue pants and one a them, whatcha callit shirts. Pull over the head kind. Shit, I don' feel so good." Her voice faded away to be replaced by the sound of retching.

Eddie turned off the recording. "That's all I got. She was pretty out of it from then on."

"She was pretty out of it the whole time," I said.

"Who do you think I can ask?" Eddie said, sounding irritated, his voice rising a couple of notches in volume. "I go asking sober people a bunch of questions like that, they're going to figure out I'm an informant." He started to pace back and forth. I couldn't blame him. He was putting himself in danger by nosing around in the affairs of drug dealers.

"I really appreciate what you've done." Having a description of a third, and possibly still alive, person of interest could be helpful, even if it came from an intoxicated source.

Eddie wouldn't give me the recording, but he agreed to save it. I gave him a couple of twenties and left him standing in the graveyard, looking a little lost. It can be very lonely for an addict who has yet to find other friends.

Something about her description of the third guy was nagging at me. A workman. Most guys who hung around with drug dealers didn't hold down a job, unless the job was directly related to the drug dealing. Some professions were more likely to be involved in drugs than others. Construction was one. You had lots of people coming and going and deliveries being made daily, as well as worksites that changed regularly. All of that provided plenty of opportunities to move drugs. For all the obvious reasons, doctors' offices and medical clinics were other prime locations for drug activity.

A vet clinic? Some of the same criteria were present—doctors, drugs and deliveries. Deliverymen wear work clothes, usually a uniform. Could that have been what she was talking about? A deliveryman would be in a good position to move drugs around. I decided to drop by Dr. Barnhill's on the way back to the office.

In the reception area was a cute Pitbull mix with a rash issue. Also waiting to be seen was a very unhappy cat with an ear infection and a strong dislike of all things veterinary. Bridget Barnhill was manning the front desk, looking worn and frustrated.

"Deputy Macklin, is there any word on Sandra?" It wasn't a secret that Sandra's real name was Kate Kelly, but it was almost impossible for any of us to stop thinking of her as Sandra.

"Not yet. I need to talk with someone who'll know about your regular delivery schedule." I wondered where Gayle was; not that I was sorry that I wouldn't have to listen to her.

"Gayle's not working today?"

Mrs. Barnhill rolled her eyes. "Her boyfriend decided that she shouldn't work here until the killer is caught."

Wayne's and Gayle's alibis had checked out. Otherwise that would have raised a huge red flag.

"The deliveries. Of course Sandra handled most of it, but I guess I would be the next person since I keep the books..." The phone rang and she held up a finger in my direction as she answered it. After helping a client make an appointment, she said, "Let me get someone up here to handle this."

She went in the back and came out a few minutes later, followed by Terry. We exchanged greetings before he sat down and took charge of the front desk.

Mrs. Barnhill walked me back to the office. "Most of our stuff comes by UPS, FedEx or the post office. The Golden Diet company has its own driver, and there's also the guy that makes those great collars and harnesses we stock out front."

I couldn't envision a grand conspiracy that included any of the nation's three main delivery services or the pet food company. But maybe a particular person...?

"Have there been any changes in drivers for the routes?"

"Again, Sandra would be the one to ask. This is really difficult. I don't know how to feel about her. Should I be worried? Or angry?"

"I don't know what to tell you. Except that it's obvious that she lied on her application, and to all of you, about who she was."

"It's so disappointing. But, you know, on one level I can understand it. There was one time in my life... You probably don't know this, but Dr. Barnhill and I had a son. He died of leukemia when he was just five years old. It almost destroyed us. Tom threw himself into his work, wouldn't talk to me. I felt like I'd lost everyone I had ever loved. And for almost a year, every day, I fantasized about changing my name, leaving everything behind and finding a new life somewhere far away."

"I think all of us have felt that way at some time in our lives," I said gently.

"But I was serious. I tried to figure out how to get a new identity. The only thing that stopped me was one day when I got up before Tom had left for work. I found him in the kitchen, crying hysterically over our boy's favorite cup. That small glimpse past his wall of denial allowed me to see that we might still have a future together." She wiped a tear from her eye. "Look at me. I'm sorry, you don't want to hear all of my troubles."

"It's all right." I gave her a minute to recover herself, then asked, "Are there any records of the deliveries?"

"Invoices. I could go back through them." She took a large binder down from a shelf.

"Go back about three months."

"What am I looking for?"

"Anything different. A new deliveryman. Problems with an order, maybe."

She started to flip through the invoices, which were all neatly punched and placed inside the book.

"Was organizing this one of Sandra's jobs?"

"She started the system and we both maintained it. I always wanted to check over the invoices. Mistakes are made. Quite a few mistakes. Most of the time someone has just put a decimal in the wrong place or mixed up one drug with another, but occasionally I think a dealer is trying to pull a fast one." Mrs. Barnhill was running her finger down each invoice with the precision of a bank teller. It was clear who kept the clinic on a sound financial footing.

"There are two different signatures for the Golden Diet pet food deliveries," she said, still scanning. "Looks like this is the regular driver." She handed me an invoice. "Then this guy came four times." She handed me another one. The name of the driver was listed as Joshua Huff.

It took her about fifteen minutes to finish scanning the rest of the paperwork, but there wasn't anything else of note.

The headquarters of the pet food company was in Alabama, but I didn't recognize the name of the city. A minute on my phone spent with Google confirmed that the company was located not more than a fifty miles from Phenix City. Was that significant?

I quickly asked the rest of the staff if they knew the delivery drivers. Dr. Barnhill was familiar with their regular driver, who also doubled as a salesman, but he'd never met Joshua Huff. The name wasn't familiar to anyone else either.

Cara walked me out to my car.

"What do you think Sandra's chances are?" she asked, but before I could answer, she continued, "I'm sorry. I know that you don't know much more than we do. I just wish I could do something to help."

I hugged her. "If I can think of anything you can do, I'll let you know."

Suddenly she gripped my arm. "Did you see that?" she asked a little too loudly next to my ear.

"What?" I turned around.

"There," she said, pointing down the road.

"I don't see anything." That wasn't strictly true. I saw plenty of cars and houses and people, but nothing that would warrant having my eardrum busted.

"It's Dad. I swear I've seen him and Mauser driving by a couple of times. This time he turned before he got close. He must have seen us out here." Cara was sounding dangerously paranoid.

"Why would he be driving past the clinic?" I asked, though I already knew the answer.

"He thinks he's protecting me," she said, sounding frustrated and maybe just a little bit grateful at the same time.

I gave her another hug and went on my way. But damned if I didn't see Henry five minutes later, driving my Dad's van with Mauser in the seat behind him, about half a mile from the clinic.

Putting crazy protective Vikings out of my mind, I tried to think of the best way to approach the pet food company.

I didn't want to spook a possible suspect when I called. I settled on the fallback position of all good detectives: I'd lie.

I called as soon as I got back to the office. "I'm doing a routine background check for the Florida Department of Motor vehicles. I need some information on your drivers."

"What kind of information?" asked the suspicious woman at Golden Diet's company headquarters.

"Nothing personal. We're just doing a routine check of commercial drivers." Repeating the script helped. "If you'd rather, I can send you some paperwork to fill out?" I said, giving her a choice I knew she'd never take.

"Okay, over the phone is fine, if it won't take long."

"Great." I proceeded to ask a lot of questions for which I had zero interest in the answers, but I needed to make it seem like I wasn't targeting any particular driver or delivery location.

Eventually, I found out what I needed to know. Huff was a relief driver and he fit the general description that Eddie's meth maiden had given us for the third man. A glance at his Alabama DMV records confirmed the resemblance. So how did he fit in?

I'd made sure that he was still employed with Golden Diet and I had a home address from the DMV records. Now the question was how to approach him. I decided to wait until I'd had a chance to talk it over with Darlene. I didn't want to spook him before we were ready.

Darlene got back to the office around three. "I've got a little surprise," she said cheerily.

"What'd you bring me?" I asked, playing along.

"Our latest victim didn't die from being run over. Well, let me rephrase that. He *might* not have died from being run over."

"He looked pretty flat to me."

"That's true. But he also had a stab wound to his heart. Dr. Darzi couldn't confirm or deny which had killed him."

"So he thinks the stabbing happened about the same

time?"

"Obviously, Watson, the knife wound had to come first. But the brutal injuries caused by the car had to have happened before, or almost before, his heart stopped."

"Wow. Not many people are killed twice in the same night."

"I asked him if someone would have had enough time to stab the guy and then get in the car and run him over. Darzi said he doubted it, but that anything's possible."

"Crazy."

I filled her in on my day.

"I like having a living suspect. Maybe we can actually bring him in and talk to him."

"That'd be a bit unusual for this case," I admitted.

"We're all over the map with this one, literally."

My phone rang. A glance at the caller ID told me it was Matt. "I'm putting you on speaker. Darlene is with me."

"Hi, Darl," Matt said, almost sounding folksy.

"Hey, Matt. Tell me you have good news for us."

"I do. I've got some dope on your runner. First off, as you've probably figured out already, this isn't the first time she's run from something. Kate Kelly's father worked for a major drug smuggler, then one day he disappeared while out on a run. Her mother died within a year of her father's disappearance. Kate hung around for a little while after that, but then she disappeared as well and no one has seen her since. One rumor going around was that the drug boss got rid of the whole family one at a time. Reasons given were the usual. They knew too much, got greedy or were going to turn state's evidence, or maybe even all three. Unfortunately, some of the people who might have known more about her have died in the last two months."

"Really? Think there's any connection?" I asked.

"In the drug business, you have these purges. This one seems to have been brought on by a stolen stash of drugs and money."

"Could that be the connection?" Darlene asked.

"Maybe. Does seem like a bit of a coincidence that they started culling the herd about the same time they went after Kate. Maybe the boss has just been tying up loose ends. A good question is: did they know where she was all along or did they get that information recently?"

"I've got an idea about that. I've got the name of a delivery guy, Joshua Huff, who works for the Golden Diet pet food company. I'll send you his information."

"I'll check it out. Does he have any priors?"

"A couple, but nothing serious."

"Sometimes they use people who have clean records to move stuff. Otherwise we could just pick up all the felons with prison tattoos and call it a day," Matt said.

"Thanks, Matt. We'll stay in touch," I said, actually sounding friendly and feeling it too.

"Okay, boys and girls, what have we learned today?" Darlene asked.

"We learned that there was a third man who is presumably still alive, who helped our two latest dead guys do whatever they were going to do to Sandra and, yes, I'm just going to keep calling her Sandra."

"And we learned that Sandra-slash-Kate has been on the run for a while."

"She was involved with some pretty nasty and dangerous people, but she got away or was allowed to leave. So is this a drug vendetta thing?"

"You should have asked our expert when you had him on the line," Darlene scolded me. "Anyway, let's not speculate yet."

"Just the facts, ma'am. Okay, we have three dead bodies and one missing woman. She may or may not have killed one or all of the victims. I think that the third man and the dog food deliveryman are one and the same," I said it with more certainty than I felt. There's the old saw about not believing in coincidences, but in the real world you see a hell of a lot of them.

"We need a list of questions to ask him."

"We can ask him about Sandra. And about his relationship to Lopez and Moreno."

"We're putting a lot of faith in your transvestite CI and his crack-addicted friend."

"Probably meth."

"Whatever. We need something solid. It may mean that we have to set up surveillance on Huff," Darlene said, causing me to cringe. Surveillance meant a judge and subpoenas, man-hours and equipment. Even if he was guilty, we might not come up with an any evidence to justify the investment.

"Maybe Matt will come up with evidence of Huff's involvement in the drug trade. Since they're already doing surveillance of some of the dealers in the Columbus area, they may have caught him on tape. That would give us some leverage." I couldn't believe that I was now relying on Matt to pull a rabbit out of his hat. "It's frustrating as hell to have half our case here and the other half a hundred miles away. And not just in other counties, but other states."

"I gave Darzi Rogers's contact info so that they can compare Lopez's wounds to Moreno's."

"I wouldn't think that Moreno's knife wound was very clearly defined, seeing as his body was run over a couple of times."

"Go ahead. Start talking about that autopsy. I think you rigged the coin toss. That body was nasty. Even Darzi's assistant had to take a break at one point. They quite literally scooped his insides out."

I grimaced. "Okay, fair enough. I won't mention the autopsy again."

"All I'll say is that Darzi is one dedicated and talented pathologist," Darlene said, looking a little green.

"Crap!" I said, sitting up.

"What?"

"Come on. We need to go see Shantel and Marcus," I said, jumping up and heading out of the office and down the hall to the evidence room.

CHAPTER TWENTY

Marcus was sorting through some boxes when we came in.

"What do you two want?" he asked suspiciously.

I held up my hands. "We aren't bringing you any more work. Jeez, you'd think that we constantly drag you out to murder scenes or something."

"More than your average bear," Marcus said. "If you're looking for Shantel, she's out helping Julio with a home invasion."

"No, you'll do fine. I just want the tire tracks from Moreno's murder scene."

"Oh!" said Darlene, with a look in her eye that told me that she was catching up with me. "Now that we know there was another man on the scene, there may have been a third car involved."

"Exactly."

Marcus had pulled up the photos on the computer and was working some magic to make some high-quality prints for me.

"Luckily the blood and guts gave us nice imprints of the tires. Though I guess it wasn't so lucky for the victim," Marcus said, sounding a bit embarrassed by his enthusiasm.

"You don't need to shed many tears for this guy. He'd

earned his bad end. Not that I won't be glad to lock his killer away for a long time."

Marcus handed me the prints.

"Okay, now that I have these, there's a software program where I can cross-check them with makes and models of cars, right?"

"Yeah," Marcus said dryly.

"Is it on all of our computers or do I have to use the ones in here? Do I need a special password for it? Don't I need the digital copies—"

Marcus rolled his eyes and grabbed the papers back out of my hands. "If you wanted me to do it, why didn't you just ask?"

"I know you're busy," I answered. "If you just give me a little help, I'm sure I can figure it out."

"It's quicker to do it myself. Get out of here," he told us. "Wait. What make and model does your prime suspect drive?"

I had to stop and consider who exactly our prime suspect was. I finally had to admit that, until we could prove that this other guy had been there, our prime suspect had to remain Sandra. I gave him the specs on her car.

"How would it change things if our mystery man killed him?" Darlene asked when we got back to our desks.

"I'm not sure. It becomes pretty damn confusing if he was helping Lopez and Moreno target Sandra, and then he turns around and runs over Moreno."

"Since the victim was run over several times, we can rule out an accident."

"Yeah… I guess. Though I'm almost not willing to rule out anything at this point. I've seen incidents where someone ran over a person by accident and then, in an effort to help, backed over them again."

"I'm not sure I could believe that in this case. But I take your point." High praise from Darlene.

"We'll have to wait for—" My phone rang.

"I got a match, but not with Sandra's car. These tires

wouldn't even fit her car," Marcus told me.

"That was fast."

"Computers, man. Back in the old days, folks had to use those old tire catalogs, holding a photo next to the book and skimming down pages trying to find a match. All I did was scan the tread into the program and press a button. Gave me, like, twenty makes and models that these tires would fit. You're looking for a small pickup truck, most likely a Ford Ranger."

I thanked him, then filled Darlene in.

"Bet you twenty dollars we find out that a pickup was stolen within a hundred and fifty miles of here."

"No bet."

We managed to pull up a list of regional car thefts and found three that fit the tires and the time frame. One had been recovered and another was stolen by a neighbor, leaving us with a black 2009 Ford Ranger stolen in Marianna, a Florida town that was between Calhoun and Phenix City if you took the back roads down to Interstate 10.

Feeling a bit of déjà vu, I asked dispatch to add an alert to the stolen truck's BOLO, noting that the vehicle was wanted in a homicide and should be preserved for evidence if anyone found it.

As it was after five and there was nothing else we could do for now, Darlene and I said our goodbyes. My phone's text alert went off as I was getting into my car. It was Cara, asking when I'd be able to get away. She didn't fool me. What she was really wondering was if she would be stuck at home alone with her parents all evening.

I pulled up next to the house just as the sun was touching the tops of the live oak trees. I didn't hear any barking and wondered if Mauser had finally gone home. Cara opened the door and Alvin came out to greet me.

Cara kissed me and rolled her eyes, letting me know that her mom and dad were inside. Also inside was Mauser, sprawled out on the floor looking like a lumpy bear rug. His chest rose and fell with a surprisingly soft snore.

"He's been running around with Henry all day," Anna said, coming out of the kitchen. "We saved dinner for you."

As usual, Anna surprised me with how good the meal was. Tonight it was a stuffed eggplant something-or-other, served with homemade bread and a better than average wine. I enjoyed the wine more than I would have thought.

"Good thing we brought a couple of bottles," Henry said as he poured the dregs of the second bottle into his glass.

The Laursens were a bit crazy, but there was a sense of peace that they carried around with them that was nice to tap into. I looked over at Cara and, from the glow in her eyes, I could tell that she was feeling as relaxed as I was. A mean-spirited part of my mind asked if I deserved to be feeling this calm and content when there was a murderer on the loose and possibly a woman in danger. Of course, the woman wasn't in danger if she was the killer. I eventually reasoned with my conscience that I would be better able to deal with the case if I had some downtime.

I fell asleep on the couch after dinner and was awakened by Cara gently shaking me.

"Wake up, sleepy-head."

"I'm awake," I lied.

"The folks have gone back to their tent," she said, settling down on the couch next to me, which suited me just fine. I wasn't ready to get up anyway. I took her hand.

"They mean well," I said, still enjoying the last of the warm glow from the wine.

"I love them. I even enjoy being around them sometimes. But their company is a little hard to take along with the murders. You need to tell my dad to stop following me around."

"Wait, why should *I* tell him to stop? Shouldn't that be your responsibility?"

"If you tell him that I'm not in danger, then he'll respect your opinion," she said, trying to sound reasonable.

"But that would be a lie."

I felt her body go tense. "Saying that doesn't help," she said, the pitch of her voice rising.

"I'm worried about you too. I can't tell him that his concern is unreasonable when it isn't," I said logically, even though I knew it wasn't the best point to make at the time.

"You just need to find Sandra and Dad needs to mind his own business," Cara said, taking her hand away from mine.

"I *am* trying to find Sandra. I'm just not sure that she wants to be found. If she's hiding, that makes my job a lot harder." There was an edge to my voice now, the mellow mood evaporating. I heard a snort and looked over my shoulder to see that Mauser was still in the house. "And why isn't he out in the teepee?"

"Dad didn't want to wake him, so I said he could sleep in here tonight."

I noticed that Alvin was tucked up in Mauser's armpit, snoring along with him. My heart softened.

"Okay, fine." I took a deep breath, trying to figure out the best course forward in the conversation. "I understand that you don't want your dad looking over your shoulder, but put yourself in his position. He cares about you and wants to be there to protect you. Is that bad?"

"I worry about him. Circling the clinic like a German Shepherd. He's going to get in an accident or something. And driving Mauser around. The poor dog is exhausted." She was trying to be serious, but one look at the monster snoozing away on the floor did not scream dog abuse.

"How many ice creams did he get?"

"Two. And that's kind of my point." But I could see the glint of humor in her eyes. One of the massive canine's redeeming qualities was his ability to make people smile. Just talking about him had lightened the mood.

"Okay, I'll talk to your dad. I'll ask him to ease up a little, but I'm not going to tell him that he doesn't have cause for concern."

"Fair enough."

I leaned forward and she leaned down and our lips met.

After a few minutes, we abandoned the living room to the dogs and Ivy and made our way to the bedroom, closing the door behind us.

On Tuesday, Darlene and I commandeered a wall of the communal office cubicles and started pasting up photos of victims, suspects and leads. We had started out in the conference room, trying to map out a way forward, but had quickly come to the conclusion that the case was too complex. We needed visual aids.

After an hour, we stepped back to admire our work. The mystery man was key, maybe *the* key. Under the heading "Mystery Man" we'd taped a copy of Joshua Huff's DMV photo and list of priors. If he *was* the mystery man, then he'd be able to provide answers to a lot of questions.

Of course, the other person who could answer a lot of questions was Sandra. We'd taped up a map of the Florida panhandle and enough of southern Georgia and Alabama to encompass all of the crime scenes and residences of our victims and witnesses. Had Sandra fled the area? If not, then her car had probably been ditched in the woods or in some body of water. We'd alerted the media to post her picture and a description of her car, listing her as an endangered woman.

"I asked IT to hack into her email and social media accounts," Darlene said.

"You got—"

"A warrant? Yes. Not hard since I could make a pretty good case that she is most likely in danger and a witness in a double homicide. Lionel didn't even have to pull out any of his superpowers. Sandra kept a pad of passwords in her desk at work."

"Which means that she probably didn't post anything too important on those accounts."

"True," Darlene allowed.

"Still, it'll be good to have the information."

"I don't think she's dumb enough to use the accounts

185

again now that she's on the run."

"We can agree on that. She's smart. I just hope she's smart enough to stay alive."

"When we find her, she's sure going to have a lot of questions to answer."

"I feel bad for John Rybeck. He appears to be the most innocent person in all of this," I said.

"Except for the fact that he was probably sent here to do something to Sandra. Oh, and that he'd been hanging around with low-life drug dealers doing God-knows-what as their enforcer."

"Sounds like he was more security than enforcer. I know, I know," I said, raising my hand as Darlene started speak, "I'm splitting hairs on that one. Everyone just liked the guy."

"Lots of people liked Ted Bundy too. Having friends does not mean you can't do bad things."

"Can't you let me have one victim here that I don't feel deserved their fate?"

"Very few people deserve to be stabbed or run over by a car or, for that matter, injected with animal tranquilizer. And whoever did it is a murderer."

"Unless," I said, "they were stabbing, running over or tranquilizing in self defense."

"True. If that's the case, then why did Miss Innocent run?"

"She couldn't face her friends and admit that she was living a lie? Or she's wanted for some other crime... or thinks she is."

"Or she doesn't trust the authorities to protect her," Darlene said thoughtfully. "Which would fit with why she ran in the first place and assumed a new identity."

"That would make Cara feel better."

"I keep forgetting how hard this must be for her."

"You remember what it was like earlier this year when we found out that one of our deputies was a killer who'd fooled us all."

"It weirded me out for a while," Darlene admitted. "We

depend on each other out there. But I can see where, even if you were just in an office setting, it would feel like a loss and a betrayal to have a friend turn out to be someone else altogether and to take off on the run."

"Cara's feeling it."

"You knew Sandra. What's your personal opinion?"

"I don't know. She seemed like a solid person. Everything about her seemed real. I didn't know her well, but still... She kept her mask on tight, I can tell you that. I think in my heart I still believe she's a good person." I shrugged. "But I've been fooled before."

I headed back to my desk. "I'm going to give Matt another call and see if he has a lead on Joshua Huff."

"Good. I'd sure like to get someone with answers into an interrogation room about now," Darlene said. "I'm going to look for more CCTV footage. There are a dozen other businesses that we can check."

I called Matt as Darlene headed out the door.

"I don't have anything for you yet. You must be desperate, calling me back so soon." There was none of the old gloating I would have expected from Matt.

"You're about right. We're hanging a lot on Huff being involved. He's pretty much our only living lead."

"I got a new intern yesterday. I put him to work going over the surveillance tapes when he came in this morning. I warn you, there are days and days of footage. We have them labeled for the major players, but this guy wasn't even on our radar."

"And he might not be involved at all. I appreciate you taking the time to go through the footage."

"No problem. I hate having to come up with work for interns. This will keep him from staring at me for a couple of days."

After talking to Matt, I called a number of law enforcement agencies within a hundred miles. BOLOs are fine, but talking personally to someone at an agency can sometimes make a difference. These days, a lot of work is done by laptop in a patrol car, but it's not impossible for information to still be entered incorrectly.

Shortly after noon, I called Cara and asked her if she wanted to go to lunch.

"We just finished up with a surgery. Give me twenty minutes."

As I got near the clinic, I saw Dad's van parked a block away with the windows rolled down. I figured this was as good a time as any to have a talk with Henry. I pulled up behind him and saw him glance in the side view mirror. He looked like a twelve-year-old caught with a beer.

I got out and walked up to the driver's side window.

"Can I help you, officer?" Henry said, doing his best to make a joke. Mauser got up and hung his head out of the window, panting at me.

"Henry, you really don't have to watch over her every second."

"I know that. But after my close call with a murderer, it isn't easy to brush this off," he said.

"You know that sitting out here is similar to how you got in trouble before." In December he'd come up here to confront someone who'd attacked a woman at the co-op he and Anna lived in. The man ended up dead and Henry became the prime suspect.

"You can't promise me she's safe."

"No, I can't. And you can't promise me that, with you sitting out here, she's any safer. We aren't even sure who's doing this. But I can tell you that you're making Cara nervous and that doesn't help."

"I know."

"Besides, Mauser isn't used to working this hard." I ruffled Mauser's ears, who rewarded me by shaking his head and showering me with dog drool.

"He's my pal," Henry said, and the big dog shifted his attention to the man who'd been gifting him with too many treats.

"Just cut it back a little."

"Okay," he said, scratching the dog's ears.

I felt bad chastising him for being a protective parent, but Cara needed the break. We said our goodbyes and I heard Henry tell Mauser that they were going to get ice cream. I sighed and drove the rest of the way to the clinic.

We had lunch at the taco stand, which made me think about Pete's recent conversation with Winston's daughter. A new restaurant in town wouldn't hurt my feelings, and Mary was a good cook.

"Still nothing," I told Cara when she asked about Sandra. "She was just too damn efficient. Most fugitives leave a ton of trash behind."

"Sandra was, I mean *is*, the most organized person I know."

"I saw the invoice books she'd maintained." A thought occurred to me. "Hey, would you like to run by her house with me real quick? Darlene and Shantel went over it, but maybe they missed something and, since you knew her better than us, you might think of something we haven't."

"Sure!" Cara said, jumping at the chance to do something productive.

Sandra's house still had crime scene tape across the door. The place was as neat as I would have expected. We searched everywhere we could think of. I even took the grill off of the air conditioner return and looked in the duct work behind the filter. Nothing. Finally, going over every inch of her mattress, I *did* find something. Or at least I found where something had probably been. The seam had been opened on the side of the mattress, leaving just enough room for a hand to reach inside. It had been neatly sewn up at each end so that the slit wouldn't open up any more than was necessary.

"That certainly looks like Sandra's work," Cara said, admiring the neat edges on the slit.

"This suggests that she came back here after the attack to get her stuff, or possibly she had a premonition that it was going to happen," I said and then realized what must have happened. "The first murder. John Rybeck. I bet you after that, she got everything ready to run if she had to."

"I hate to think that she knew why that man had been killed and didn't say anything," Cara said.

"Remember, she could be his killer. I know that's hard to accept."

"If she knew she might have to run, then you won't find anything here. Sandra would have cleaned up everything."

"You're right."

After another twenty minutes, we gave up and headed back to the clinic. As I dropped Cara off, there was no sign of Henry or Mauser.

CHAPTER TWENTY-ONE

Back at the office, I got a call from Beth in the records department.

"If you want to come down here, I've got something for you." For a moment my mouth watered at the thought of some of her baked treats, but then I remembered that I'd asked her to do a records search on Sandra.

Beth handed me a few sheets of paper when I got to her desk.

"I'm pretty sure that's your woman. Age is close and the name is Kelly Strom. She even used the numbers from some of her other addresses when making up the false one on this document." Beth pointed to a copy of a purchase agreement. "She used a realtor here in town as kind of a blind agent. He never saw her. They just communicated over the phone. The phone number is there. I was tempted to try it, but I'd bet a bushel of apples it's no good. None of the real estate closing was done in person."

The top piece of paper was a copy of a deed. On another sheet was the description of the parcel, and the last sheet was a copy of a map from the property appraiser's website showing the parcel's location. The date was two-and-a-half years ago, not long after she'd come to town.

"Great!" I looked down at the property appraiser's information, which showed that the land was vacant with no structures. Taxes were paid up. "I'll check it out."

"You owe me," Beth said good-naturedly, but I got the feeling she meant to collect.

I called Darlene and told her where I was headed.

"You want me to ride along?"

"No sense both of us going. According to everything I've seen, there isn't even a house on the land. So the odds that she's hiding out there are pretty slim. The place is down in the southwest corner of the county."

"Sandhill country," Darlene said, referring to the part of Adams County that was more sand than fertile soil, left over from tens of thousands of years ago when the gulf waters were lapping at our hills. Now the land grew only pine trees, turkey oaks and gopher tortoises.

I drove for twenty minutes before I passed the last of the pasture land and the ground became sandier and well drained. Most of the land in this part of the county was owned by timber interests who used it to grow pine trees that were harvested and turned into pulp wood. They'd clear-cut the land, plant slash pine, wait ten or fifteen years, then clear-cut it again.

There weren't many houses out here and all of the side roads were unpaved. I found my first turn and drove slowly down the road, sending clouds of dust into the air behind me. The road rolled through the ancient dunes until I found my second turn. Half a mile after that, I came to a place where a new culvert had been installed, making a simple driveway over the drainage ditch that ran parallel to the road.

Three strands of barbed wire on metal posts ran off from each side of the driveway and a metal gate was padlocked shut. I parked my car in the drive and climbed over the gate. According to the property appraiser's records, the parcel was twenty acres. The woods were thin and open—just pine trees and palmettos.

A driveway had been bulldozed all the way back to a large

cleared area. In some spots, I could still see the dozer tracks. I guessed that it had been done about the same time the culvert had been installed. This land was so poor that only wiregrass and palmetto grew well, so very little underbrush had grown up since the driveway had been cleared. I didn't need to walk the entire property as I could see most of it by walking a couple of hundred feet down the sandy drive. It was impossible to tell when the last car had driven down the road since the sand was so loose. Each time I lifted my foot, the sand slid back into my tracks, covering them up again.

Sandra might have had plans to put a structure out here, but it looked like she'd never gotten the chance. I turned around and climbed the gate back out, stopping to examine the padlock. It appeared to be in good working order. She'd been smart and sprayed oil on it. Again, there was no way of telling when it had last been opened. Driving out here had been a waste of time. I sighed and returned to my car.

As I passed into the Calhoun city limits, my phone rang. It was Cara.

"What's up?"

"I've got an idea."

"About what?"

"One of the things we were looking for at her house were receipts so you could get an idea of what she had been buying before she disappeared, right?"

"Yeah."

"I've got a way to find out what she was buying, or at least what she was thinking about buying." Cara could barely contain the excitement in her voice.

"I'm all ears," I said, smiling to myself.

"I want to show you."

"Okay."

"We may need whoever you use for IT stuff."

"Can you get off work and meet me at the sheriff's office?"

"I'll be there by four-thirty."

Darlene still hadn't returned by the time I got back to the

office. I texted her and told her that I'd struck out at Sandra's property. She texted back that she was still out looking at CCTV footage from different businesses, still hoping to catch another sight of Sandra's car or the mystery Ford Ranger.

Cara arrived a few minutes later, looking excited.

"I was thinking about Sandra and looking at my Facebook page. As usual, I was getting annoyed at all the stupid ads. That's when it hit me, 'cause you said that your IT guy had gotten onto her Facebook page and email accounts." She rattled this off excitedly.

"So…" I said, but almost before it was out of my mouth I had figured it out. "Facebook ads are tied to your browsing history."

"That's right. And it's tied to the account so you don't need her computer. It's not about the computer, it's about the account." Cara's eyes glowed with satisfaction and I was beginning to catch her enthusiasm for the idea.

I called Lionel to confirm that he was in his office, then Cara followed me down the hall to the small room next to our dispatch office. Since he was expecting us, I opened the door and walked in. The room wasn't that small, but since it was crammed with servers and duct work it seemed small. The temperature was a brisk sixty-eight degrees and the air was full of the steady hum of machines at work.

Lionel stood up when we came in. He was bundled up in a parka.

"The only way I can keep from freezing to death," he said to Cara when he saw her looking at the parka. I introduced them and Cara told him about her idea.

"Yeah, that's good thinking. I should have thought of it. The ads will definitely give you some idea of what she'd been cruising for on the Internet. Here, I can bring up her accounts." He sat down at his desk, which held three large monitors arranged in a semicircle.

He hit a few keys at a blinding pace, referring now and again to a notebook where he'd written down Sandra's passwords. In a matter of seconds, each of the three screens showed a different account. On the first was Sandra's Facebook account. I saw Cara listed as one of her friends. I looked over at Cara and saw her face turning red as she stared at the blue and white page containing so many lies that she and her colleagues had so willingly believed.

The second screen held Sandra's email account and the third screen showed an Amazon account in her name. I'd already reviewed her order history, which had consisted mostly of romance novels.

Now I scanned all three of the web pages and did something unnatural. I focused not on the content, but on the ads.

"I'm taking screenshots," Lionel told me as all three of us peered intently at the content.

"Weird," Cara said.

"Interesting," I mumbled. Most of the ads on Facebook were for Tallahassee-area land clearing and heavy equipment operators. One of the small ads was for a military surplus company. At the bottom of her email page there was an ad for cargo containers like the ones used to store bulk items on cargo ships. That ad stayed up for a minute and then switched to one for industrial equipment.

"Am I right in assuming that, if these companies don't have a specific account to base their ads on, they would just use the demographic information of the user to generate the ads?"

"Basically. It's all done with algorithms. They gather information, whatever is available, and then the algorithms spit out the ads that are best targeted to the user," Lionel said.

"And if all they had was Sandra's demographic data—a woman in her thirties living in north Florida, working as an officer manager—all of that would probably get chewed up and the ads we'd see would be for professional women's clothes, maybe a car or vacation."

"That's right. I see where you're going. What we're seeing

must be based on something other than her basic demographic information."

"Exactly!"

"But what does it mean?" Cara asked. "She wasn't building anything."

"Actually, there was evidence that she'd had someone clear part of her land."

"So she searched for a land clearing company and now we're seeing ads for construction companies. I guess that makes sense."

"And here is an ad for MREs from an outdoor sports retail company," Lionel pointed out.

"So you think she was planning to camp out at her place?" Cara asked me.

"Maybe. Drug smugglers use all kinds of survival equipment for various reasons." As I watched, the ad for the MREs changed to one for shovels, which seemed somewhat ominous since she was connected to several murders. I wondered if anyone else had gone missing. "Can you record all of this?" I asked Lionel.

"Sure. I'll move them all to one screen and record it. I'll leave it up and scroll or refresh the pages occasionally so new ads will pop up. I've got an upgrade to perform on several of the servers tonight, so I'll be here for a while."

"Thanks, Lionel."

Cara and I left him to his work and headed to the parking lot.

"I guess that didn't get us too far," Cara said, sounding a little down after the initial excitement of following her lead.

"I don't know about that. It painted a little different picture of Sandra than what I'd had in my head."

"Is that a good thing?"

"That's a very good thing if the new picture is more accurate. Besides trying to find Sandra, and beyond solving these murders, I need to catch the killer so your parents will pull up their yurt and go home." I bumped into her playfully.

"Tell me about it. Between Dad following me around and

Mom constantly in our kitchen, I'm going mad."

"We all go a little mad sometimes," I said, doing my best Norman Bates impression.

"I'm glad you can joke about them."

"They're good people, and they care about you. I can't be too mad at them."

"You're right. Dad just needs to turn off his inner sheepdog. It's distracting to look in my rearview mirror and see him following me."

"Just ignore him as best you can. Don't look in your rearview mirror any more than you have to," I said, not knowing that this suggestion would come back to bite me in the ass.

"I'll try."

"Believe me, I look forward to helping them pack up the yurt. Have you broke it to your dad that he can't take Mauser home with him?"

"He's going to cry," she said with a chuckle.

"Mauser or your father?"

"Both."

We parted company at the parking lot. I went to find Darlene while Cara headed home.

Darlene was sitting in the back of the In and Out liquor store, looking like she'd been on her own drinking bender.

"If I see one more flickering black-and-white image, I'm either going to go blind or puke," she told me as I pulled up a chair next to her. "I swear, if I win the lottery I'm going to buy every business in this one-horse town some brand-spanking-new, state-of-the-art color digital closed-circuit systems."

"Make sure you buy them new computers and software with facial recognition and car tag identification capabilities too," I told her.

"Damn, that's a good idea, son," she complimented me while keeping her blurry eyes on the monitor.

"Found anything?"

She stopped the playback and picked up her notebook.

"A blurry car headed south on Jefferson. Could have been Sandra's car. Too blurry to tell who was driving. That was at the Fast Mart. There were a couple of others, but the times seemed off. The best thing I got was this." She pulled out a printout of a man. "This is a man who was near Lopez's car about an hour before the attack. Camera is at the Express Burger. Lopez and Moreno got a late lunch there. This guy comes at the car from a far corner of the parking lot. Unfortunately, his car is too far away from the building to be picked up by the camera. This is zoomed in. Maybe Lionel or one of the other guys can clean it up, but I doubt it. The camera they've got must have been installed when the Bee Gees were at the top of the charts."

"He looks a little like our guy with the dog food company," I said, though honestly the photo was so grainy that it looked like half the guys in the county.

"Not much to hang your hat on," Darlene admitted.

"We're pretty much just fishing right now," I said, mixing up the metaphors.

"I hope we catch something soon."

"How much more do you have to do?"

"I'm going an hour on both sides of the murder. I just passed the halfway point. I should be done here in half an hour. Oh, and I asked the woman and the guy who were working that day if they'd seen Lopez or Moreno. I thought there was a chance they might have stopped in for some liquid courage. But it was a no go."

"Are you done after this?"

"I'm about done in now. So, yeah, I'm going to call it a day."

I stayed with her for moral support while she went through the last of the video.

It was mercifully quiet when I got home. Cara, Ivy and Alvin were the only ones waiting for me inside.

"All quiet on the yurt front?"

"Dad spent all day doing whatever, and Mom built us a

compost pile out of old pallets. They were both tired. I heard all three of them snoring after they had an early dinner." Cara smiled and I gave her a hug until I felt Ivy reaching out from a chair to pull on my shirt.

"Oh, I see, if there's no one around to give you treats then you want my attention. I don't know about that," I said, gently scratching the tabby's ears.

We settled down to a quiet evening, but something kept nagging at the back of my mind. I felt like there was a clue right in front of me that I couldn't quite see. Every time I started to relax, a sense of urgency would kick in, telling me that I knew the answer to where Sandra could be.

"What?" Cara asked at one point, when she caught me staring off at the windows instead of watching TV heroes fight their way out of another tight spot.

"I don't know," I said. "I think I've seen some pieces of the puzzle and can't quite remember what they are."

"Something to do with Sandra?"

"Or the murders. But, yeah, I think Sandra."

"Does it have to do with the ads?"

"Yes, no, maybe. It's like when you know a name, but can't quite come up with it."

"Just relax and try not to force the answer out. Let your subconscious work on finding the pieces," Cara said and snuggled up against me. I put my arm around her and tried to relax.

I managed to forget about my mental roadblock for a little while so that Cara and I were able to fully enjoy the fact that we had an evening to ourselves. After making love, we took a shower and found ourselves in bed at a reasonable hour.

I slept until about five the next morning. I got up and stumbled to the bathroom, planning to come back and get another hour's sleep, when I realized what had been bothering me, what I'd seen and how it fit in with what I knew.

Half of me wanted that additional hour of sleep, but I

knew it wasn't going to happen. I shaved, brushed my teeth and got dressed quietly so that I wouldn't wake Cara.

I fed Ivy and Alvin, who were thrilled that I'd gotten up so early. I forced myself to sit down at the table and eat my bowl of cereal. I would at least let the sun come up. I used some of the time to do a little research on my laptop. There were three companies in Adams County that provided earth-moving services and another seven in Tallahassee. I would expand the search if those companies didn't bear fruit.

By six-thirty the world had taken on the blueish light of early dawn and I decided that it was time to go. I looked in on Cara, who was just waking up.

"You off already?" she mumbled.

"I want to check on something before going to the office. I'll give you a call if I find anything interesting."

CHAPTER TWENTY-TWO

When I came out of the house, I saw Henry walking with Mauser. Henry waved to me while Mauser glanced up with the bleary-eyed stare of someone who didn't want to be out of bed yet. I thought that the dog was going to need a couple days of rest whenever Henry and Anna finally went home.

On the way to my car I made a quick detour to the toolshed, grabbing a four-foot-long piece of rebar that had been used as a survey stake when I bought the property.

I was at Sandra's property half an hour later. Everything appeared to be the same, though the glare from the rising sun made it tough to see into the shadows. I climbed the gate again, holding my piece of rebar, and walked down the driveway to the cleared area near the center of the property.

The clearing, including the crest of a small sandy ridge, was about an acre or an acre and a half square. This morning, I started at one corner and walked slowly, dropping the rebar against the ground every two yards or so. I was halfway across the clearing when I saw an odd clump of weeds. Palmetto and wiregrass had started to grow up across the area, but in this one spot there was a bit more than anywhere else. I decided to abandon my methodical grid pattern and investigate.

The spot was about three feet square. There was a large clump of wiregrass with other non-native grasses mixed in with it. It looked like someone had planted them. I took my piece of rebar and dropped it in the middle of the clump. The resulting sound was hollow and wooden.

I got down on my knees and started digging around the edges of the grass, discovering that the clump was surrounded by wood. This was, for all intents and purposes, a planter. In fifteen minutes, I'd cleared all around the edges. The wooden planter was set down inside a larger wooden frame. I felt around, eventually finding small finger-sized cut-outs on either side of the planter's base. I lifted and was able to pull the planter up and slide it out of the way.

Underneath was a square hole that went down two feet to a metal surface. I took my flashlight out of my pocket and got my head down inside the hole. The piece of metal looked like it slid back along one side. I reached down and tried to move the lid, but it wouldn't budge. Next, I took my piece of rebar and tapped it on the metal. As I'd suspected, the sound was hollow.

"You need to come out. I'm Deputy Larry Macklin with the Adams County Sheriff's Office." There was no response and I wondered if I was simply talking to myself. I tried calling out a couple more times, listening closely for the sound of any movement from below. Still nothing.

I'd managed to put together the fact that Sandra might have buried a cargo container on her property and that she could have been using it either for storage or to actually live in. I'd seen some articles on survivalists who were doing this as cheap prepper retreats. I should have put it together as soon as I saw the ads for cargo containers pop up on her web pages. The question now: was Sandra hiding out in the container? Of course, another possibility was that someone had killed her and left her body in there.

I thought about my options. The makeshift hatch seemed to be secured on the inside, which suggested that Sandra, or someone, was inside. If I called for backup, we would end up cutting our way in, which might only end in a bloody confrontation. I wanted to try something else first.

I took out my phone. Out here in the far reaches of the county, cell towers were few and far between. I wasn't getting much of a signal. I moved back to the gate and got a tenuous bar and a half.

I leaned against the gate and tried to think through the possibilities. I couldn't see a big downside to calling Cara and having her come out there. Maybe she could reassure Sandra if she was down in the cargo container. If we could talk her into coming out, it would be better for everyone. What would an hour one way or the other matter? If Cara didn't get a response, then I would call in the cavalry and have them cut their way in.

I speed-dialed Cara.

"Hey, what's up?"

"I've got something here you might be able to help with."

"What? You're breaking up."

I climbed up on the gate and tried to get a little elevation. "Better?"

"Yeah, what's going on? Where are you?"

"I'm at Sandra's property. I think you might be able to help me with something." I didn't want her worrying and over-thinking everything as she drove out. There would be plenty of time to explain once she was here. "Can you come out?"

"I guess. Let me check with Dr. Barnhill." She was gone for a minute, then said, "I'll be there in about twenty minutes. What's this all about?"

"I'll tell you when you get here. I'll text you the address. Google maps will get you here."

I paced off the rest of the area while I was waiting. I found what appeared to be the air supply about twenty yards from where I'd found the entrance to the container. The opening was well protected by a clump of Spanish bayonets that had been planted around it. The only way a person could get close to the opening would be to chop down the plants.

Grimly, I considered the possibility that we might have to smoke out whoever was inside if they wouldn't come out voluntarily. Smoke them out or use a torch to cut our way in. Both options seemed dangerous. Hopefully, we wouldn't have to resort to either of those more dramatic choices.

Cara pulled up to the gate and was out of the car and waiting for me by the time I got there.

"I guess I climb over?" she asked. Being a gentleman, I held out my hand to help her up and over.

"So what do you need me for?" Cara looked around, clearly unimpressed.

"There is a cargo container buried over here," I said, already moving in the direction of the hatch.

"What?" Cara said, sounding more confused. I couldn't blame her.

"Here," I said, standing by the hole in the ground.

"There's one of those huge things that you see on trains buried *here*?"

"I'm pretty sure. Sandra bought the land and then had a company bury a cargo container."

"That's mad. Not that I don't know people that have lived in them. I remember one of the communes we lived in when I was a kid had a whole section where people had put a couple of them together and then made them into homes. Some people had done a better job than others. But none of them were buried." She kneeled down and peered into the hole. "How does the door work?"

"I'm not a hundred percent sure about that. I think it slides to the side. Looks like someone welded brackets for it."

"Have you tried to open it?" she asked and I was forced to bite my tongue and not hit her with all of the sarcastic answers that immediately sprang to mind.

"Yes. I didn't have any luck."

"She sure went to a lot of trouble. You think she's here?" She almost whispered the last part as though she didn't want

Sandra to hear her, which was exactly the opposite of why I'd asked her to come out.

"I think there's a chance. I didn't want to call out the SWAT team yet. I thought if you came out here, then you could ask her to come out. She'll probably trust you more than me or a bunch of cops."

"Now?"

"Please."

Cara looked doubtful, but called out, "Sandra, are you down there? It's Cara." Silence. "I'm here with my boyfriend, Larry. You know him. We just want to help."

"Sandra, we know most of the story now. We know your real name is Kate Kelly. We know all of this has something to do with drugs and your past in Columbus, Georgia. I promise you that, if you come out now, I will do everything I can to help you," I added.

"Dr. Barnhill and everyone at the clinic has been worried to death about you," Cara said, looking at me as though wondering if she was getting it right. I shrugged my shoulders. Who knew what would or wouldn't work. "Larry knows that those guys who came after you were dangerous. If you were just protecting yourself, everyone will understand."

That's when we heard a sound from below. Just one slight bang. We waited, but there was nothing else.

"I know it's easy to get caught up in something that gets out of control. We really want to help you," I yelled down into the hole.

Then I turned to Cara and whispered, "Ask her to just say something so that we know she's all right."

Cara nodded. "Sandra, please, just say something. It would be a huge relief just knowing you're okay."

I looked at Cara, putting my finger over my lips. I wanted to give Sandra lots of time to think about this.

A minute feels twice as long when you're just waiting for someone to respond. I let a minute drag into two minutes.

"I'm fine," a woman's voice finally said from the other

side of the hatch.

Cara smiled at me. "I am so glad to hear your voice. We were so worried!"

I made the shushing sign again and we waited some more.

"Damn it! Why did you have to find me?" Sandra eventually said. "They'll kill me."

"Who?" Cara asked.

"It's a very long story."

"Larry will help you. He can protect you." It felt good to hear her say that.

"Ha! I don't think he can."

"I have a friend with the DEA. We really can help you." I couldn't believe that I'd just referred to Matt as a friend. Strange bedfellows and all. "We know you were close to some pretty bad people."

"They're going to want me to testify. If I agree to that, I will die."

"The U.S. Marshals will be charged with keeping you safe."

"Whatever."

"Look, let's talk face to face. This shouting at each other isn't the best way to have a conversation," I pleaded.

"I'm not going to come out and be arrested."

"I'll make a deal with you. Come out and we'll talk for half an hour. If you want to go back down after that, then I won't stop you."

Sandra was quiet again.

"You can trust Larry. I promise you, he'll do what he says."

After a few minutes, we finally heard a rattling noise at the hatch. Slowly it slid back. Sandra, blinking and looking disheveled, stared up at us like an astronaut looking out on a strange new planet.

Cara and I stood up and backed away. Slowly, Sandra clambered out of the hole. She was dressed in dirty jeans and a T-shirt. She hardly looked like the same professionally dressed and composed woman that I'd seen at the clinic.

"Thank you," I said.

"Let's make this quick. I'm not—Who the hell is that?!" she suddenly barked in alarm, pointing past me. Cara and I both turned instinctively. Afterward I thought how stupid that was. Sandra could have been playing the oldest trick in the book. But when I turned, I thought I saw just the slightest hint of movement.

The gate was far enough away that I could barely make out the outline of our cars parked behind it. There were just enough trees and underbrush in the uncleared area to make it hard to see them clearly.

"Get down," I told Cara and Sandra. We all squatted down by the hole. *Did she really see someone out there or not?* I wondered. I might have just seen the movement of a bird or a squirrel. On the other hand, there were some very dangerous people on the hunt for Sandra. If I could find this property, then they could too. I pulled out my phone and confirmed that there was still no service.

"You all get down in the hole. I'm going to see who's here. And, if necessary, I'll sneak up to my car and call for backup." I didn't like the idea of Cara going down into the container with someone who might or might not be dangerous, but if some of the men that were hunting Sandra were on the property, then up here definitely wasn't safe.

Sandra was already crawling back into the hole.

"Be careful," Cara said, putting her hand on my arm, then she followed Sandra down into the dark.

CHAPTER TWENTY-THREE

As soon as the lid slid shut, I took out my gun and started walking away from the cleared drive. I wanted to see who was there without being seen myself. I headed for a thick area of palmettos on the west side of the drive. Of course, I still had to keep my eye out. If Sandra had seen bad guys, then they wouldn't want to walk down the cleared drive either. They would have seen the cars and would know that someone else was here, so I'd need to cut a wide path back to the gate.

Palmettos always made me think about rattlesnakes. I couldn't help keeping one eye on the ground as I made my way up a narrow deer path. Finally, about fifty yards from the gate, I saw a man with a gun sneaking down my side of the drive. He was about ten feet from the drive and about thirty feet from my deer path.

I only got a quick look at his face, but I recognized him. It was Joshua Huff, the pet food deliveryman. I watched him as he crept through the underbrush. He was still about ten feet closer to the cars than I was. I crouched down behind a palmetto and decided to let him pass so I could make my way to the gate and call for backup. He couldn't get to Sandra and Cara, so there was no harm in letting him discover the hole.

That's when fate intervened. Fate or a weak bladder. Huff stopped and looked around. When he'd satisfied himself that no one else was close by, he moved toward me. Without seeing me, he put his gun back inside the holster in his waistband, unzipped his pants and began to pee.

I had to make a quick decision, but this one seemed like a no-brainer. I stood up and pointed my gun at him.

"Keep your dick in your hands and don't move," I told him. He stared at me and I could see the wheels turning inside his head. "Don't do it. I swear to you there is no way that you can possibly pull your gun without me putting at least two holes into you first. If you're finished, put yourself back in your pants and zip up very, very slowly."

He did as he was told.

"Who are you?" he asked and I realized that I'd just screwed up Cop 101.

"Sorry," I said politely, still feeling smug about capturing our number one suspect so easily. "I'm a deputy with the Adams County Sheriff's Office. Now turn and walk very slowly to the clearing. And if you make any sudden moves, I *will* shoot you."

We made our way into the clearing, where I had him remove his gun with two fingers while he faced away from me and dropped it on the ground. I then had him walk forward before asking him to lie down and put his hands behind his back so that I could cuff him.

"Joshua Huff, I'm arresting you for trespassing on private property." It was the only charge for which I was absolutely sure I had just cause. I read him his rights, then looked back toward the cars. I could go and call for backup now, but that would be betraying Sandra's trust. Besides, I wanted to get Cara out of that cargo container as soon as I could. So I made the decision to take my prisoner and go back to the hole to let them know that everything was okay.

I marched Huff down to the hole.

"What the hell is this?" he asked. From the look on his

face, I could tell that he thought I might be planning to kill and bury him.

I took the piece of rebar and tapped on the hatch. "Cara, it's okay. You can come out," I yelled down into the hole. As I waited for an answer that didn't come, I wondered if something was wrong. Had I made a mistake by sending Cara down into the container with Sandra? But, to my relief, the hatch slid open moments later. Cara was the first to come up out of the hole with Sandra following cautiously.

"You!" Sandra said accusingly to Huff. "Who the hell are you, and why are you doing this to me?" She started toward him with her fists curled, but I got in between them.

"There'll be time enough for accusations later. Sandra, you need to come back with us," I said to her. "I know this man's involved, but I need your statements to help figure this all out."

"You're going to listen to her?" Huff shouted. "She's going to lie through her teeth to save herself."

"Don't give me that crap. You killed those men!" Sandra shouted back.

"I was saving your life!"

"Sandra, do you see how important it is that you come back with us? If I take him in without you, he's going to tell his story first. It would be much better if we had yours to compare it to," I tried to reason with her. I could see that she was thinking about it.

"Oh, shit!" Huff suddenly exclaimed in a hushed and panicked voice. "Let me go, let me go. We got to get out of here, fast!" Huff was dancing around and throwing his head as if he was having a fit.

"What—" I started to say.

"They. Will. Kill. All. Of. Us!" he said, his eyes almost popping from their sockets and his head still jerking.

I turned toward the cleared driveway and saw them. They were still eighty yards away, but I could see there were at least four men and at least two of them were armed with rifles. They were drug dealers straight out of central casting.

I only had a moment to decide what to do. I was out-numbered and out-gunned. Plus, I had the responsibility of protecting two civilians and a prisoner.

"Get back in the hole. Go, go!" I said to Sandra, Cara and Huff. I had to pull Huff back when he tried to push his way to the front of the line. "Ladies first," I growled.

Just as I glanced back, a shot rang out and sand flew up into the air just five feet from the hole. "Hurry!" I urged.

Sandra went first, followed by Cara. I had to hold Huff back to keep him from pushing Cara down the ladder. I pulled my gun as Huff started down into the hole. Two more shots rang out, one striking a foot away while the other whizzed overhead. As I turned to climb into the hole, I fired a couple of wild shots in the attackers' direction. They scattered, giving me time to get down into the hole.

Once I cleared the hatch, I scrambled to close it. There was a metal bar to secure the hatch and prevent anyone up top from sliding it open. As I moved down the ladder, I realized thankfully that the room was not completely dark. A soft glow came from a battery-powered lantern sitting on a table.

We were all breathing hard. The air was damp and stale. In the dim light, I saw Sandra make her way over to the wall and turn on a small fan.

"It brings in some outside air," she explained when she saw me looking at her.

The room's dimensions were standard for a shipping container—eight feet wide, eight-and-a-half feet high and forty feet long. There was a bed at one end and a small table and chair at the other. A recliner, several coolers and various boxes took up the rest of the space. The metal ladder we'd come down on was in the middle of the room.

"Nice place," I said a little too harshly. Just then the pounding started on the hatch. Everyone jumped.

"Don't worry, they can't get through," Sandra said. I hoped she was right. Knowing there was no point, I took out my phone and checked for a signal.

I named my service provider. "Anyone have anything different?" I asked. In the county, we'd all learned that some providers gave better coverage than others depending on where you were at any time.

"I do. My phone's in my pocket," Huff said, pushing out his hip. The phone was clearly outlined. I took my gun out of the holster where I'd returned it before closing the hatch. I handed it to Cara before walking over to Huff. I reached into his pocket and pulled out his phone. Swiping it open, I saw the "no service" message up at the top.

"I could have told you that," Sandra said. "I wasn't thinking about cell service when I bought this land."

"I won't ask you why you bought it. That's pretty obvious. You knew when you took the job at the vet that you might need a hideout someday."

"I did."

The pounding continued. I thought we could all use the distraction of conversation.

"What are you running from?"

"Ha! That's a long story."

"I think we have time."

"I guess. Hell, have a seat." She gestured at the meager furniture selection. I moved the handcuffed Huff to the chair by the table while Sandra dropped into the old recliner. I took my gun back from Cara and we settled side by side on the edge of the bed.

"Why?" Cara asked her.

"I don't even know when it started. I was just a kid. My dad was a pilot. Flew helicopters in the military, but he could fly anything. Unfortunately, he got in trouble when he was in his thirties. Drunk driving offense. Someone was hurt. Not too bad, but the DUI was enough to guarantee that he couldn't get a real job flying for anyone. He told me that he just sort of ended up flying for a gang of drug dealers."

"Where was your mother?"

"She was there. She pretended that Dad worked as an aircraft mechanic. Which was true, but that wasn't what was funding our lifestyle. Which was pretty darn nice. We lived in Columbus in a beautiful subdivision surrounded by lawyers and doctors. I went to the best schools. I can understand how my parents convinced themselves that they were doing the right thing."

"Did you know?" I asked.

"Not at first. I guess I was sixteen or seventeen when I started to figure things out."

"What was that like?" Cara wanted to know.

"It was odd. The man Dad worked for was—well, is—a legitimate businessman. At least he is part of the time. The rest of the time he's a drug smuggler and dealer. But everything looked on the up-and-up from the outside. Eventually, I even began dating his son. Then one day Dad went on one of his trips and never came back. This was about five years ago. Mom lasted about a year before committing suicide by alcohol. I was so tight with the boss's family at that point, and a user myself, that for a while I thought I could just go on like nothing had happened. But one day it dawned on me that these people had killed my father and mother. They may not have been directly involved, but still... The way they had sucked my father in, and the people they worked with, all of that had contributed to his death. I knew that, if I stayed, sooner or later the lifestyle would kill me too."

"Those kind of people don't just let you walk away," I said.

"That's true. And I knew that too. But Troy, the boss's son, was different. I don't think he wanted to be there any more than I did. And, by this time, he and I were more friends than lovers. He agreed to run interference for me with his family. His father agreed that if I disappeared, then he wouldn't look for me."

"That was all it took?" I asked, not believing they'd let her go that easily.

"That was the gist of it. What actually happened was that the father took me to a room in a warehouse in a part of town where I had never been before. He tied me up and stood over me with a knife. He said, 'Remember how helpless you feel right now. If I ever hear your name again, I will bring you back here and unspeakable things will happen to you.' He told me that he had informers everywhere and that if he heard that I had so much as sat down next to a DEA agent, or shook hands with someone employed by the FBI, he'd know."

"I guess you believed him."

"I knew what he said was true. And all I wanted was to get away. To reinvent myself."

"So you came here," Cara said.

"I did. I could have moved a lot farther away, but distance didn't mean much. I thought I'd be safer in surroundings that felt familiar."

"You did all of this yourself?" I asked.

"Actually, I had help from one of Dad's old friends. A mechanic that he worked with. I guess he's kind of my unofficial godfather. He's a great welder. He did the hatch and helped me to set up the air exchange and the charger."

"Charger?"

"I've got a line that leads to some camouflaged solar panels. I can charge batteries and do a few things like that."

"Where's the bathroom?" I'd just noticed that one important feature was missing.

Sandra got up and went over to one side of the container, where a panel I hadn't previously noticed had been cut. There were a couple of thumbscrews holding it in place.

"Through here is another container. I had three of them buried, two side by side and one perpendicular to the second one. The next one over has a chemical toilet and supplies."

"Three?" Cara asked.

"From the next one over you can open another panel and go into the third one. We're on a hill and the doors on that one open to the outside. I have my smart car parked in there."

Relief flooded over me. "So we can get out through those

doors?"

"No. We can't. Once I parked my car inside, I closed the doors and then covered them up with sand. It took me a whole day. Since the doors of the shipping container open out, there's no way we can push them open."

"Great," I said. "You thought of everything except for how to get out."

"I figured that if someone found me then I wouldn't want to get out," Sandra said bluntly.

"So what happened? Why did they come for you now?" Cara asked, currently more interested in Sandra's problems than in our own.

"I honestly don't know," Sandra said, sounding baffled. She pointed an accusatory finger at Huff. "He has something to do with it. You look familiar. I think you know what this is all about."

"Good point," I said, staring at Huff. "Why don't you tell us what part you've played in all of this."

"I don't think so."

"Okay, maybe we can negotiate a deal with the guys on the outside. They might be glad to get you."

"You wouldn't do that."

"If it comes down to a trade for Cara's and Sandra's lives, then you're gone. I wouldn't hesitate," I said and he could read the truth in my eyes.

"If I told you the truth, then you'd be even more likely to throw me out to the wolves."

"Maybe, maybe not. Actually, I don't need you to tell me what you did. I bet I can figure it out."

Huff looked skeptical, so I turned to Sandra. "Let's work on John Rybeck's murder. Had you ever seen him before?" I asked her.

"No. I didn't know anything about him until he was found dead."

"Did anything odd happen before that? Like a letter or a phone call?"

"I did get a strange email from someone who said that he

wanted to talk to me. I thought it was some creeper. But it was a day before the murder."

"I don't think John was going to hurt you. I think he wanted to talk with you first." I turned to Huff. "Which means that you killed him, not to prevent him from killing Sandra but just the opposite. You killed him because he *wasn't* going to kill her." I saw his eyes shift and knew that I was on the right track.

I asked Sandra to tell us what had happened when Lopez and Moreno attacked her.

"I was being cautious. I wasn't completely sure that the first murder was because of me, but it seemed the most likely possibility. I know I should have said something then, but you really couldn't protect me from these people."

"There will be plenty of time for regrets," I told her.

"I had a gun in my purse and was prepared to use it. When I left the clinic, I locked the door and got down the steps before these two guys jumped out at me. One of them grabbed me from behind. He must have been hiding around the side of the building and snuck up behind me. I dropped my purse, trying to get my gun. They were dragging me to a car when another guy, him," she said, pointing at Huff, "must have come up behind the guy who was holding me. I realized later that he'd stabbed the guy. I broke loose and he yelled for me to run. I managed to grab my keys and my gun and stumbled to my car. When I looked back, all three of them were fighting. When I was backing out, the second guy, the one who had been helping the first to abduct me, was running off. This guy," again she pointed at Huff, "was getting off of the ground."

"Was the guy who grabbed you dead?" I asked.

"No, he was trying to crawl on his hands and knees in the parking lot."

"I saved her life!" Huff crowed. "Killing someone in defense of another person isn't a crime."

"Running him over is what's going to make you hang. Oh, yeah, and hunting down the third man. Of course,

216

killing Rybeck will probably get you the cold-blooded killer award all by itself."

"You can't prove most of that," Huff said, sulking.

"I'm betting the State Attorney will be able to prove ninety-five percent of it. We have tire tracks. You probably left some DNA on the syringe or on Rybeck's body. And I'm willing to wager that we can tie you to the murder of Lopez as well."

"Why are you all after me?" Sandra asked.

"He saw you when he made a delivery. You recognized her, didn't you?"

"Whatever," he grumbled.

"You said you thought he looked familiar. He made four deliveries to the vet. Had you seen him before that?" I asked Sandra.

She looked at him more closely. "You're right! He made some of the Golden Diet deliveries. I thought that he was acting strange at the time. He'd never look me in the eye. But before that...? Maybe. There was a guy who used to hang around the boss's house when I was with Troy. This guy was always trying to be one of the regulars. Almost begging to go with them."

"Screw you," he said.

"You recognized her, but you didn't tell your boss right away. You had a plan. What was it? It required Sandra to stay on the run, didn't it? But you miscalculated."

"She didn't have to stay on the run, but she couldn't be allowed to run her mouth. They might believe her. If that asshole John would have just killed her then everything would have been fine. But he wanted to talk to her. Try and help her. How the hell did he even get to be one of their enforcers? I had to trick him into meeting me that night at the vet."

"How did you get in?"

"I'd planned it all out during my deliveries. I thought a break-in at the vet might spook her into running, so I'd planted a small camera on the dog food rack. It's across from the alarm system so I could get the code on video. And I swiped an extra key that hung near the back door when I was bringing in food. I just didn't plan on Rybeck showing up and forcing my hand."

Cursing the vet's poor security in my head, I said, "Okay, then what the hell was up with the bag of blood?"

He shook his head sadly. "John was an idiot. I told him that the clinic was hiding drugs in the blood bags. I handed him one of the bags so that his hands would be full when I made my move with the syringe."

"Congratulations. I never would have guessed that. But as for your motive, you blamed something on her, didn't you? What was it? Drugs or money? You may as well tell us 'cause you'll never get near it. Either these guys," I pointed up to where we could still hear the men trying to get through the hatch, "will kill you or you're going to jail for the rest of your life. And I have a feeling that when I let it be known that you were framing Sandra for something you did, word will get back to the bosses and your life in jail will be very short."

"You can't do that. I'll need to be protected in jail." He was beginning to see his dilemma.

"Either you make friends in here right now or you face the full wrath of your former employer out there."

"Money and drugs. A total of a hundred million dollars. Half a million of it went to a man who I convinced to describe Kate Kelly as the woman who stole it. I dropped a couple more clues and let the boss figure it out for himself. But I didn't know they'd find her so soon. I was going to spook her, get her to run and then kill her. Afterward, I'd get rid of the body where no one would ever find it. Her and the drugs and the money would all just seem to disappear." He paused and looked at Sandra. "Nothing personal. I just needed you to disappear in a way that made it look like you were running. Who the hell would have thought you'd have your own redneck bomb shelter?"

"How'd you find out about my shelter?" Sandra asked.

"I didn't. I followed her this morning," he said, pointing to Cara. "For once, Frankenstein and his dog weren't following her."

"I wasn't looking behind me," Cara said, sounding embarrassed. "You told me not to keep looking behind me." She glanced at me pathetically.

"Guilty," I said to Cara. "So you convinced the dealer that Sandra stole the drugs?" I asked Huff.

"That's right. I'd been trying to see how to get my hands on a drop-off for a while. When I saw Kate at the vet, it all clicked. She was the perfect patsy. They remembered her and everyone knew that she had enough knowledge of the operation to pull off something like that. After the heist, everyone was on the warpath looking for her. When they found her, and don't ask me how they found her, I stepped in and offered to help bring her in. They trusted me."

"Great. I think your friends must have stopped trusting you," I said, pointing to the pounding on the hatch.

"I had to use one of their phones to lure Lopez down the dirt road. He was hurt bad after that night, but he wasn't dying fast enough. He didn't know if I was working alone or with others, so he was scared to just come back to Columbus. I stole one of the boss's phones and texted him to meet me on that dirt road. Someone must have gotten suspicious and they followed me. Hell, now they probably think I was working with the bitch."

"They could have put a tracking device on your car or phone. It would be easy enough."

"What now?" Cara asked. "Will Darlene come looking for us?"

"Eventually, but I didn't tell anyone I was coming out here. I've got a tracking device on my car for dispatch, so they'll ultimately be able to find us. But the goons up there might find the air intake before that happens. When they do, they can just smoke us out. We need to get help sooner rather than later."

"There *is* a way out," Sandra said, causing all of us to turn and look at her. "Maybe," she added.

"Where?" I asked, standing up. "We probably don't have much time." I realized that I hadn't heard any noise from the hatch for a few minutes.

"In the container that has my car." Sandra got up and led me to the hole into the other container. I took out my flashlight and led the way into the bathroom and storage container. Then I stopped. "Wait. Do you have any duct tape?"

Sandra dug out a roll and I went back through the hole into the main container.

"Hey, come on, you can't do this," Huff said as I proceeded to tape him up.

"If you shut up, I won't tape your mouth," I told him. There was no way I was going to leave him restrained only by a pair of handcuffs. A person could do a lot of damage, even wearing cuffs. He quit protesting as I taped his legs together and his arms down at his sides.

"I'm determined to get you safely to the sheriff's office where you can then be booked in on multiple charges of murder. That should be a comfort considering the alternatives." There was extra emphasis put on this last part by the renewed cursing and pounding coming from the overhead hatch. It sounded like they'd found something very heavy to use against the steel. I just hoped they'd continue to concentrate on the hatch and not realize that there had to be air vents.

I quickly went back through the hole and into the other container where Sandra was waiting for me. No sooner had I gotten through than I heard Cara behind me. "I'm coming too."

Sandra uncovered the opening to the container where her car was hidden. I looked through the hole and saw the front of her car and more boxes. I went through, followed by Sandra and Cara.

"My dad's friend put a larger air vent in this container because of the car. It's still small, but not that long. At the end is a fan, which is off right now. On the other side of the fan is a grate that's secured from this side. You should be able to unscrew the grate and push the fan and the grate out ahead of you."

I looked through the hole and could see daylight about fifteen feet away through the fan. It would be a very tight squeeze for me. Easier for Sandra or Cara, but that wasn't an option.

"Okay," I said, not feeling very sure at all. I took off my gun and set it down in the tunnel in front of me, doing the same with my flashlight and a screwdriver that Sandra handed to me. There wouldn't be any way for me to get my hands down to my sides once I was inside the small tunnel. I started to squeeze in, but my shirt kept snagging on the edges. I took it off. "It might help if I was wet," I said.

"I've got a better idea." Sandra disappeared back into the other container.

"I hate to leave you alone with those two," I told Cara.

"I still trust Sandra. I'm scared for you." She hugged me tightly.

"I have to go. We don't know how long we'll have before those knuckleheads start looking around for the air vents. Once I'm out, I'm going to make my way to the cars and call for help." I didn't tell her that I planned on drawing the drug thugs away once I made the call for help. I planned to make a lot of noise, then drive off in my car. They wouldn't know that it was just me and, by all rights, that should cause them to forget about the hatch and what was below and chase after me. At least that was the plan.

Sandra came back, holding a large bottle of cooking oil.

"You have got to be kidding!"

CHAPTER TWENTY-FOUR

Cara reached out and took the bottle from Sandra. She wiped the oil all over my shoulders, arms and torso, slowing gently as she reached the angry scar on my left side. Luckily, my hips weren't too wide, so I could keep my pants on.

"That's good," I said and gave Cara a quick kiss. Then I leaned down and slipped into the duct work.

I hated to admit it, but the oil helped. Unfortunately, there was just enough sand in the tunnel to make it a painful and abrasive crawl down to the end. Once I got there I was glad that I had my flashlight. The light coming in from the grate created just enough glare to make it difficult to see the screw heads. Luckily, there were only two screws holding the fan in place.

With the fan unscrewed, I was able to push it close enough to the grate that I could reach the grate screws as well. By this point my arms were aching from the awkward position and sweat was dripping down into my eyes.

After what felt like hours, but was probably no more than ten minutes, I was able to push the fan and grate out of the end of the duct work. I tried to make as little noise as possible. I groaned silently as I saw the obstacle course of Spanish bayonets that awaited my bare skin.

I took a deep breath. There was nothing to do but go for it. I pushed the flashlight out ahead of me, then thought about the screwdriver. It wasn't much of a weapon, but it could still come in handy. I put the rubber end in my mouth since I couldn't yet reach my pockets. I grabbed my gun, then pushed myself out of the tunnel and onto the cruel, pointed ends of the wicked plants.

I was lucky to have the screwdriver in my mouth to bite off the screams as the needle ends of the plants poked and scraped my face, chest, hands and sides. I pulled myself across the plants until my feet were finally free, then rolled away from the hill and the source of my pain. I can only imagine what kind of demented castaway pirate I must have resembled, with my shirt off and rivulets of blood streaming down my oiled chest as I clutched a gun in one hand and held the screwdriver clenched in my teeth.

I took the screwdriver out of my mouth and put it in my pocket. I looked around, listening intently. Loud conversation was coming from up on the sand hill. I pulled out my phone on the off chance that I might get a signal, but no such luck.

I started to move away and around the side of the hill. Now I could hear the voices more clearly. They had begun to search for another way in. I was halfway around the hill when I heard someone shout, "There!" I didn't have to look to know that they were pointing at me. I started running for all I was worth. At one point I tripped over some palmettos and went down, but I was back on my feet without ever having come to a standstill.

My mind was racing almost as fast as my feet. *Should I try for the cleared drive where I can run faster and have less chance of tripping, or stay in the brush?* A couple of shots rang out, helping to make up my mind. I'd present less of a target in the brush, and if I did go down, I'd still have a chance of hiding.

Panting and running, with no time to look around, I could hear them shouting behind me. What was I going to do when I got to the road? If I could find a place to hide, or could put some distance between myself and my pursuers, I would be able to use my phone. But I couldn't run at full speed and still dial the phone. Precious seconds would be lost as I got my phone out of my pocket and looked down to dial.

I could see two of the men in my peripheral vision now as they passed me seventy feet over on the cleared track. Those that had followed me into the brush weren't catching up, but now I couldn't head toward the cars. I started to veer away from the cleared drive, the gate and the cars. I was still heading toward the dirt road, but I'd have to go over the three strands of barbed wire.

I could see the fence twenty feet ahead of me, but I couldn't see the two guys who'd headed toward the gate anymore.

"We got him! He's coming to the fence," I heard one of the guys behind me yell.

When I was close to the fence I wheeled around and fired two shots in their direction. The shots were wild and un-aimed, but they served their purpose, causing the two guys chasing me to reconsider their next moves.

I turned back to the fence. I had only one choice. I threw myself over the barbed wire, adding more bloody tracks to my skin, and landed on the other side. I hit the sandy culvert and rolled down it, regaining my feet faster then I would have thought possible. I was up on the road and headed away from the cars and back toward town. My only hope was to be able to jump back into the woods at some point, hide and call 911.

I was pounding down the road when I heard a car start up, its engine racing behind me. One or both of the men who'd gone to the gate had been smart enough to get in a car. My options were narrowing fast. I could only assume that the men I'd shot at had recovered and were clambering over the fence and in pursuit again. With men on foot close by and a car roaring down on me from behind, I didn't stand much of a chance.

I decided that before the car caught up to me, I'd turn and fight it out. If I could do enough damage, I might buy some time for Cara and Sandra. Plus, I'd leave a solid crime scene for Darlene, Pete, Shantel and Marcus to follow up on and be able to string these bastards up.

My side was aching and my throat burning as I ran down the road. That's when I saw another vehicle parked alongside the road about hundred feet ahead of me. Maybe it was a hunter tending to his feed plot. Only pigs and varmints were in season right now. I began to pray that someone was near the vehicle and willing and able to help.

I heard the car speeding up behind me. I didn't think I could make it to the one in front of me before the one in back ran me down. I would have to jump the ditch and go into the woods. But just before I made my move for the side of the road, I saw the other vehicle, a van, start up and come toward me. The van and I were closing on each other fast. If I hadn't been exhausted and in flight mode, my mouth would have fallen open. It was Dad's van and Henry was behind the wheel, picking up speed rather than slowing down.

I could hear the car behind me and knew it had to be close. Henry was going head-to-head with it in a game of chicken and I was in the middle. I dove into the ditch, my fingers crossed that Henry knew what he was doing.

I heard vehicles swerving and huge clouds of dust swept over me from both directions. I heard metal scrapping metal, then the sound of a car going into the ditch. I stood quickly and was relieved to see the car that had been chasing me roll into the pine trees. I came up out of the ditch and saw the brake lights on the van as it slid to a stop. I ran toward it, wasting no time with hellos as I yanked the passenger door open and climbed in.

"Go, go, go!" I shouted, trying to pull the door closed as Henry accelerated. A couple of gunshots rang out as we sped past the gate.

"Where's Cara?" Henry yelled.

"She'll be fine for a while," I said, pulling out my phone and seeing a blessed signal. I called 911, identified myself and gave them details, then I had them patch me through to Darlene and I told her to get Pete and bring the cavalry. I wanted more than a couple of patrol officers. I also gave Darlene the list of roads that they needed to barricade in order to keep the roaches from scurrying back into the woodwork.

A loud *woof* from the back of the van told me that Mauser was claiming his role as part of the team that had rescued me.

Henry, Mauser and I were standing by the hatch when Cara and Sandra climbed up out of the hole. There were hugs all around before Darlene and I went down, un-taped Huff and hauled him up to the surface.

By the time I got back to the office, Matt was waiting for me. I could tell that he was resisting making a comment about my appearance. I was still partially covered in oil and sand and wearing an old T-shirt I'd had in my car. Between the oil and the blood, I hadn't wanted to ruin my button-down shirt after I'd recovered it from the container.

"I want to take a couple of your suspects," Matt said.

"Not Huff," I told him flatly.

"Not Huff. One of the guys who came at you at the property is a pretty big fish. We have a chance to flip him."

"Take them." I really didn't care about anyone else but Huff and Sandra.

"I also want to talk Kate Kelly into entering the witness protection program."

"You can talk to her. But no thumbscrew tactics on her."

"Don't worry. We need her to be a friendly witness."

He went on to tell me that he thought they had the story confined to the group we had captured. If he moved quickly, he thought he'd be able to use the stolen money and drugs to bait a trap for some of the others.

"The story will get out fast," I said.

"I know. That's why I also need to interview Huff before I leave. If I come down hard on him, he should sing."

"Works for me," I said, enjoying the idea of Huff getting swatted for what he knew about the operation. "As long as I can burn him for the murders."

"Give me two days, max, and you can do what you want with him. We'll give you everything we have on him to make your case," Matt said.

Greenlighted, Matt headed for the jail to get to work on Huff.

Darlene came in after supervising the clean-up at the property.

"We sealed the place off," she said, dropping into a chair. "What were you doing running off on your own like that? You know better." Darlene scolded me like a parent would a child.

"I had a hunch. I didn't know it would get that interesting that fast. Anyway, you were probably wasting your time collecting evidence out there. The thugs are going with Matt, and Sandra-Kate will get to walk if she agrees to enter the witness protection program."

"You okay with that?" Darlene asked

"I'm actually glad that we don't to have to decide whether to prosecute her or not."

"How are you? You'll want to use some aloe on those scratches," Darlene said sympathetically.

"I'll survive."

"You've had a rough couple of months. You've earned a vacation."

"I hear that."

We talked about the reports that would have to be written and agreed that they could all wait until tomorrow. Darlene had already talked to the State Attorney and had done all of the paperwork needed to keep Huff locked up until his hearing that was scheduled for Friday morning.

It was dark by the time I drove into my yard and saw a campfire burning cheerily by the yurt. I was greeted by a happy group that included Cara, Mauser, Alvin, Dad, Genie, Henry and Anna.

"Seriously, you really don't have to throw yourself into harm's way every chance you get," Dad chastised me. I was pretty sure that I could hear a little pride in his voice, but that might have just been the bourbon he was nursing.

Cara hugged me as I shook Henry's hand and ruffled Mauser's ears.

"So tell me, how did you two end up out there?" I asked.

"He put a locator app on my phone," Cara said with only a little exasperation in her voice.

"After you told me that I was making her nervous, I called a friend who has a teenage son and asked him to recommend a tracking program. It was pretty easy to install."

"He put it on my phone yesterday afternoon when I wasn't looking." Cara was trying to sound mad, but it was hard to be angry at someone who had probably saved all of our lives.

"When I realized she'd left work, I tracked her out there. I saw the cars and thought you were meeting with other cops, so the big guy and I just parked and watched," he said, petting Mauser as the dog leaned into him.

"Don't think I'm putting you two on the payroll," Dad said. "Speaking of work, you should really take a vacation," he said to me.

Holding Cara close to my side, and feeling all of the aches and pains of the day start to settle in, I thought that Dad and Darlene might just have a point.

Larry Macklin returns in:

June's Troubles
A Larry Macklin Mystery–Book 8

ACKNOWLEDGMENTS

In addition to everyone included in the dedication, there's one more veterinarian deserving of my thanks. Dr. Tom Whitley's willingness to employ my wife as a kennel tech many, many years ago has provided much of the inspiration for Cara's work experiences—minus the murder, but definitely including the reference to pulling a cat off of her head that she makes in *April's Desires*.

As always, I have to recognize the amazing and constant support and encouragement I've received from H. Y. Hanna, as well as her original cover design. Words cannot express my appreciation for all her help.

If you can have one thing in life, choose luck. I was very lucky indeed to have met a woman who could be my friend, my editor and my wife. Much of what I've accomplished, including this series, could not have been done without Melanie.

Original Cover Concept by H. Y. Hanna
Cover Design by Robin Ludwig Design Inc.
www.gobookcoverdesign.com

ABOUT THE AUTHOR

A. E. Howe lives and writes on a farm in the wilds of north Florida with his wife, horses and more cats than he can count. He received a degree in English Education from the University of Georgia and is a produced screenwriter and playwright. His first published book was *Broken State*; the Larry Macklin Mysteries is his first series and he has plans for more. Howe is also the co-host of the "Guns of Hollywood" podcast, part of the Firearms Radio Network. When not writing or podcasting, Howe enjoys riding, competitive shooting and working on the farm.

Made in the USA
Middletown, DE
08 September 2022